"I'm thinking about you too much. It's not the way I used to think about you."

"Times change," Frederica said unsteadily. "So do people."

"You don't always want them to, and it's not always for the best. This isn't for the best," Nick murmured as he lowered his mouth to hers. The images that spun through his brain aroused him, amazed him, appalled him.

"I lied," he said, pulling back. "I said I wouldn't touch you again."

"I want you to touch me."

"I know." He kept his hands firm on her shoulders. "What I want is for you to go home, back to your hotel, now."

"You want me to stay," she whispered. "You want to be with me."

"No, I don't." That, at least, was the truth. He didn't want it, even if he seemed so violently to need it. "We're practically family, Fred, and it looks as though we may be working together. I'm not going to ruin that. Neither are you."

"All right, I'll wait." She started for the door, then turned. "But you're still going to think about me, Nick, too much. And it's never going to be the way it used to be again."

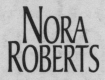

NORA ROBERTS

WAITING FOR NICK

Silhouette

SPECIAL EDITION™

Published by Silhouette Books

America's Publisher of Contemporary Romance

For the family

 SILHOUETTE BOOKS

ISBN 0-373-23996-3

WAITING FOR NICK

Visit Silhouette at www.eHarlequin.com

Printed in U.S.A.

WAITING FOR NICK

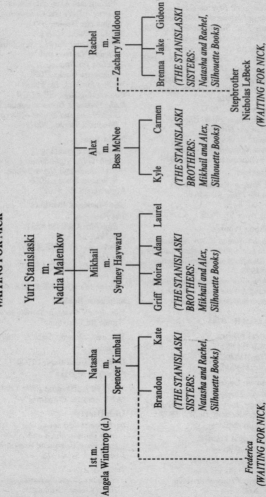

Yuri Stanislaski
m.
Nadia Malenkov

Natasha
1st m.
Angela Winthrop (d.)
m.
Spencer Kimball

Mikhail
m.
Sydney Hayward

Alex
m.
Bess McNee

Rachel
m.
Zachary Muldoon

Brandon   Kate

*(THE STANISLASKI
SISTERS:
Natasha and Rachel,
Silhouette Books)*

Griff   Moira   Adam   Laurel

*(THE STANISLASKI
BROTHERS:
Mikhail and Alex,
Silhouette Books)*

Kyle   Carmen

*(THE STANISLASKI
BROTHERS:
Mikhail and Alex,
Silhouette Books)*

Brenna   Jake   Gideon

*(THE STANISLASKI
SISTERS:
Natasha and Rachel,
Silhouette Books)*

Stepbrother
Nicholas LeBeck
*(WAITING FOR NICK,
Silhouette Special Edition)*

Frederica
*(WAITING FOR NICK,
Silhouette Special Edition)*

Chapter One

She was a woman with a mission. Her move from West Virginia to New York had a series of purposes, outlined carefully in her mind. She would find the perfect place to live, become a success in her chosen field, and get her man.

Preferably, but not necessarily, in that order.

Frederica Kimball was, she liked to think, a flexible woman.

As she walked down the sidewalk on the East Side in the early-spring twilight, she thought of home. The house in Shepherdstown, West Virginia, with her parents and siblings, was, to Freddie's mind, the perfect place to live. Rambling, noisy, full of music and voices.

She doubted that she could have left it if she

hadn't known she would always be welcomed back with open arms.

It was true that she had been to New York many times, and had ties there, as well, but she already missed the familiar—her own room, tucked into the second story of the old stone house, the love and companionship of her siblings, her father's music, her mother's laugh.

But she wasn't a child any longer. She was twenty-four, and long past the age to begin to make her own.

In any case, she reminded herself, she was very much at home in Manhattan. After all, she'd spent the first few years of her life there. And much of her life in the years after had included visits—but all with family, she acknowledged.

Well, this time, she thought, straightening her shoulders, she was on her own. And she had a job to do. The first order of business would be to convince a certain Nicholas LeBeck that he needed a partner.

The success and reputation he'd accumulated as a composer over the past few years would only increase with her beside him as his lyricist. Already, just by closing her eyes and projecting, she could envision the LeBeck-Kimball name in lights on the Great White Way. She had only to let her imagination bloom to have the music they would write flow like a river through her head.

Now all she had to do, she thought with a wry smile, was convince Nick to see and hear the same thing.

She could, if necessary, use family loyalty to persuade him. They were, in a roundabout way, semi-cousins.

Kissing cousins, she thought now, while her eyes lighted with a smile. That was her final and most vital mission. Before she was done, Nick would fall as desperately in love with her as she was, had always been, with him.

She'd waited ten years for him, and that, to Freddie's mind, was quite long enough.

It's past time, Nick, she decided, tugging on the hem of her royal blue blazer, to face your fate.

Still, nerves warred with confidence as she stood outside the door of Lower the Boom. The popular neighborhood bar belonged to Zack Muldoon, Nick's brother. Stepbrother, technically, but Freddie's family had always been more into affection than termi-nology. The fact that Zack had married Freddie's stepmother's sister made the Stanislaski-Muldoon-Kimball-LeBeck families one convoluted clan.

Freddie's longtime dream had been to forge another loop in that family chain, linking her and Nick.

She took a deep breath, tugged on her blazer again, ran her hands over the reddish-gold mop of curls she could never quite tame and wished once, hopelessly, that she had just a dash of the Stanislaskis' exotic good looks. Then she reached for the door.

She'd make do with what she had, and make damned sure it was enough.

The air in Lower the Boom carried the yeasty

scent of beer, overlaid with the rich, spicy scent of marinara. Freddie decided that Rio, Zack's longtime cook, must have a pasta special going. On the juke, Dion was warning his fellow man about the fickle heart of Runaround Sue.

Everything was there, everything in place, the cozy paneled walls, the seafaring motif of brass bells and nautical gear, the long, scarred bar and the gleaming glassware. But no Nick. Still, she smiled as she walked to the bar and slid onto a padded stool.

"Buy me a drink, sailor?"

Distracted, Zack glanced up from drawing a draft. His easy smile widened instantly into a grin. "Freddie—hey! I didn't think you were coming in until the end of the week."

"I like surprises."

"I like this kind." Expertly Zack slid the mug of beer down the bar so that it braked between the waiting hands of his patron. Then he leaned over, caught Freddie's face in both of his big hands and gave her a loud, smacking kiss. "Pretty as ever."

"You, too."

And he was, she thought. In the ten years since she'd met him, he'd only improved, like good whiskey, with age. The dark hair was still thick and curling, and the deep blue eyes were magnetic. And his face, she thought with a sigh. Tanned, tough, with laugh lines only enhancing its character and charm.

More than once in her life, Freddie had wondered how it was that she was surrounded by physically stunning people. "How's Rachel?"

"Her Honor is terrific."

Freddie's lips curved at the use of the title, and the affection behind it. Zack's wife—her aunt—was now a criminal court judge. "We're all so proud of her. Did you see the trick gavel Mama sent her? The one that makes this crashing-glass sound when you bop something with it?"

"Seen it?" His grin was quick and crooked. "She bops me with it regularly. It's something, having a judge in the family." His eyes twinkled. "And she looks fabulous in those black robes."

"I bet. How about the kids?"

"The terrible trio? They're great. Want a soda?"

Amused, Freddie tilted her head. "What, are you going to card me, Zack? I'm twenty-four, remember?"

Rubbing his chin, he studied her. The small build and china-doll skin would probably always be deceiving. If he hadn't known her age, as well as the age of his own children, he would have asked for ID.

"I just can't take it in. Little Freddie, all grown up."

"Since I am—" she crossed her legs and settled in "—why don't you pour me a white wine?"

"Coming up." Long experience had him reaching behind him for the proper glass without looking. "How're your folks, the kids?"

"Everybody's good, and everyone sends their love." She took the glass Zack handed her and lifted it in a toast. "To family."

Zack tapped a squat bottle of mineral water against her glass. "So what are your plans, honey?"

"Oh, I've got a few of them." She smiled into her wine before she sipped. And wondered what he would think if she mentioned that the biggest plan of her life was to woo his younger brother. "The first is to find an apartment."

"You know you can stay with us as long as you want."

"I know. Or with Grandma and Papa, or Mikhail and Sydney, or Alex and Bess." She smiled again. It was a comfort to know she was surrounded by people who loved her. But… "I really want a place of my own." She propped her elbow on the bar. "It's time, I think, for a little adventure." When he started to speak, she grinned and shook her head at him. "You're not going to lecture, are you, Uncle Zack? Not you, the boy who went to sea."

She had him there, he thought. He'd been a great deal younger than twenty-four when he shipped out for the first time. "Okay, no lecture. But I'm keeping my eye on you."

"I'm counting on it." Freddie sat back and rocked a little on the stool, then asked—casually, she hoped—"So, what's Nick up to? I thought I might run into him here."

"He's around. In the kitchen, I think, shoveling in some of Rio's pasta special."

She sniffed the air for effect. "Smells great. I think I'll wander on back and say hi."

"Go ahead. And tell Nick we're waiting for him to play for his supper."

"I'll do that."

She carried her wine with her and firmly resisted the urge to fuss with her hair or tug on her jacket again. Her attitude toward her looks was one of resignation. 'Cute' was the best she'd ever been able to do with her combination of small build and slight stature. Long ago she'd given up on the fantasy that she would blossom into anything that could be termed lush or glamorous.

Added to a petite figure was madly curling hair that was caught somewhere between gold and red, a dusting of freckles over a pert nose, wide gray eyes, and dimples. In her teenage years, she'd pined for sleek and sophisticated. Or wild and wanton. Curvy and cunning. Freddie liked to think that, with maturity, she'd accepted herself as she was.

But there were still moments when she mourned being a life-size Kewpie doll in a family of Renaissance sculptures.

Then again, she reminded herself, if she wanted Nick to take her seriously as a woman, she had to take herself seriously first.

With that in mind, she pushed open the kitchen door. And her heart jolted straight into her throat.

There was nothing she could do about it. It had been the same every time she saw him, from the first time she'd seen him to the last. Everything she'd ever wanted, everything she'd ever dreamed of, was sitting at the kitchen table, hunkered over a plate of fettuccine marinara.

Nicholas LeBeck, the bad boy her aunt Rachel had defended with passion and conviction in the courts. The troubled youth who had been guided away from the violence of street gangs and back alleys by love and care and the discipline of family.

He was a man now, but he still carried some of the rebellion and wildness of his youth. In his eyes, she thought, her pulse humming. Those wonderful stormy green eyes. He still wore his hair long, pulled back into a stubby ponytail of dark, bronzed blond. He had a poet's mouth, a boxer's chin, and the hands of an artist.

She'd spent many nights fantasizing about those long-fingered, wide-palmed hands. Once she got beyond the face, with its fascinating hint of cheekbones and its slightly crooked nose—broken years ago by her own sharp line drive, which he'd tried unsuccessfully to field—she could, with pleasure, move on.

He was built like a runner, long, rangy, and wore old gray jeans, white at the knees. His shirtsleeves were rolled up to the elbow and missing a button.

As he ate, he carried on a running commentary with the huge black cook, while Rio shook the grease out of a basket of french fries.

"I didn't say there was too much garlic. I said I like a lot of garlic." Nick forked in another bite as if to back up his statement. "Getting pretty damned temperamental in your old age, pal," Nick added, his voice slightly muffled by the generous amount of pasta he'd just swallowed.

Rio's mild, good-natured oath carried the music of the islands. "Don't tell me about old, skinny boy—I can still beat hell out of you."

"I'm shaking." Grinning, Nick broke off a hunk of garlic bread just as Freddie let the door swing shut behind her. His eyes lighted with pleasure as he dropped the bread again and pushed back from the table. "Hey, Rio, look who's here. How's it going, Fred?"

He crossed over to give her a casual, brotherly hug. Then his brows drew together as the body that pressed firmly against his reminded him, uncomfortably, that little Fred was a woman.

"Ah…" He backed off, still smiling, but his hands dipped cautiously into his pockets. "I thought you were coming in later in the week."

"I changed my mind." Her confidence lifted a full notch at his reaction. "Hi, Rio." Freddie set her wineglass aside so that she could properly return the bear hug she was enveloped in.

"Little doll. Sit down and eat."

"I think I will. I thought about your cooking, Rio, all the way up on the train." She sat, smiled and held out a hand to Nick. "Come sit down, your food's getting cold."

"Yeah." He took her hand, gave it a quick squeeze, then let it go as he settled beside her. "So, how is everybody? Brandon still kicking butt on the baseball diamond?"

"Batting .420, leading the high school league in home runs and RBIs." She let out a long sigh as Rio set a large plate in front of her. "Katie's last ballet recital was really lovely. Mama cried, of course, but then she tears up when Brand hits a four-bagger. You know, her toy store was just featured in the *Washington Post*. And Dad's just finishing a new composition." She twirled pasta onto her fork. "So, how are things with you?"

"They're fine."

"Working on anything?"

"I've got another Broadway thing coming up." He shrugged. It was still hard for him to let people know when something mattered.

"You should have won the Tony for *Last Stop*."

"Being nominated was cool."

She shook her head. It wasn't enough for him— or for her. "It was a fabulous score, Nick. *Is* a fabulous score," she corrected, since the musical was still playing to full houses. "We're all so proud of you."

"Well. It's a living."

"Don't make his head bigger than it is," Rio warned from his stove.

"Hey, I caught you humming 'This Once,'" Nick noted with a grin.

Rio moved his massive shoulders in dismissal. "So, maybe one or two of the tunes weren't bad. Eat."

"Are you working with anyone yet?" Freddie asked. "On the new score?"

"No. It's just in the preliminary stages. I've hardly gotten started myself."

That was exactly what she'd wanted to hear. "I read somewhere that Michael Lorrey was committed to another project. You'll need a new lyricist."

"Yeah." Nick frowned as he scooped up more pasta. "It's too bad. I liked working with him. There are too many people out there who don't hear the music, just their own words."

"That would be a problem," Freddie agreed, clearing a path for herself. "You need someone with a solid music background, who hears words in the melody."

"Exactly." He picked up his beer and started to drink.

"What you need, Nick, is me." Freddie said firmly.

Nick swallowed hastily, set his beer down and looked at Freddie as though she had suddenly stopped speaking English. "Huh?"

"I've been studying music all my life." It was a struggle, but she kept the eagerness out of her voice and spoke matter-of-factly. "One of my first memories is of sitting on my father's lap, with his hands over mine on the piano keys. But, to his disappointment, composing isn't my first love. Words are. I could write your words, Nick, better than anyone else." Her eyes, gray and calm and smiling, met his. "Because I not only understand your music, I understand you. So what do you think?"

He shifted in his chair, blew out a breath. "I don't know what to think, Fred. This is kind of out of left field."

"I don't know why. You know I've written lyrics for some of Dad's compositions. And a few others besides." She broke off a piece of bread, chewed it thoughtfully. "It seems to me to be a very logical, comfortable solution all around. I'm looking for work, you're looking for a lyricist."

"Yeah." But it made him nervous, the idea of working with her. To be honest, he'd have had to admit that in the past few years, *she'd* begun to make him nervous.

"So you'll think about it." She smiled again, knowing, as the member of a large family, the strategic value of an apparent retreat. "And if you start to like the idea, you can run it by the producers."

"I could do that," Nick said slowly. "Sure, I could do that."

"Great. I'll be coming around here off and on, or you can reach me at the Waldorf."

"The Waldorf? Why are you staying at a hotel?"

"Just temporarily, until I find an apartment. You don't know of anything in the area, do you? I like this neighborhood."

"No, I—I didn't realize you were making this permanent." His brows knit again. "I mean, a really permanent move."

"Well, I am. And no, before you start, I'm not going to stay with the family. I'm going to find out what it's like to live alone. You're still upstairs, right? In Zack's old place?"

"That's right."

"So, if you hear about anything in the neighborhood, you'll let me know."

It surprised him that even for a moment he would worry about what her moving to New York would change in his life. Of course, it wouldn't change anything at all.

"I picture you more Park Avenue."

"I lived on Park Avenue once," she said, finishing up the last of her fettuccine. "I'm looking for something else." And, she thought, wouldn't it be handy if she found a place close to his? She pushed her hair out of her face and tipped back in her chair. "Rio, that was sensational. If I find a place close by, I'll be in here for dinner every night."

"Maybe we'll kick Nick out and you can move upstairs." He winked at her. "I'd rather look at you than his ugly face."

"Well, in the meantime—" she rose and kissed Rio's scarred cheek "—Zack wants you to come out when you're done Nick, and play."

"I'll be out in a minute."

"I'll tell him. Maybe I'll hang around for a little while and listen. Bye, Rio."

"Bye, doll," Rio whistled a tune as he moved back to his stove. "Little Freddie's all grown up. Pretty as a picture."

"Yeah, she's okay." Nick resented the fact that whatever spicy scent she'd been wearing was tugging on his senses like a baited hook. "Still wide-eyed, though. She doesn't have a clue what she's going to face in this town, in this business."

"So, you'll look out for her," Rio thwacked a wooden spoon against his huge palm. "Or I look out for you."

"Big talk." Nick snagged his bottle of beer and sauntered out.

One of Freddie's favorite things about New York was that she could walk two blocks in any given direction and see something new. A dress in a bou-

tique, a face in the crowd, a hustler looking for
marks. She was, she knew, naive in some ways—in
the ways a woman might be when she had been
raised with love and care in a small town. She could
never claim to have Nick's street smarts, but she felt
she had a good solid dose of common sense. She
used it to plan her first full day in the city.

Nibbling on her breakfast croissant, she studied
the view of the city from her hotel window. There
was a great deal she wanted to accomplish. A visit
to her uncle Mikhail at his art gallery would down
two birds. She could catch up with him and see if
his wife, Sydney, might know of any available apart-
ments through her real estate connections.

And it wouldn't hurt to drop a bug in his ear—
and the ears of other family members—that she was
hoping to work with Nick on his latest score.

Not really fair, Fred, she told herself, and poured
a second cup of coffee. But love didn't always take
fair into account. And she would never have applied
even this type of benign pressure if she wasn't confident in her own talents. As far as her skill with
music and lyrics was concerned, Freddie was more
than sure of herself. It was only when it came to her
ability to attract Nick that she faltered.

But surely, once they were working so closely
together, he would stop seeing her as his little cousin
from West Virginia. She'd never be able to compete
head-on with the sultry, striking women he drew to
him. So, Freddie thought, nodding to herself, she'd
be sneaky, and wind her way into his heart through
their shared love of music.

It was all for his own good, after all. She was the best thing in the world for him. All she had to do was make him realize it.

Since there was no time like the present, she pushed away from the table and hurried into the bedroom to dress.

An hour later, Freddie climbed out of a cab in front of a SoHo gallery. It was a fifty-fifty shot as to whether she'd find her uncle in. He was just as likely to be at his and Sydney's Connecticut home, sculpting or playing with their children. It was every bit as likely he might be helping his father with some carpentry job, anywhere in the city.

With a shrug, Freddie pulled open the beveled-glass door. If she missed Mikhail here, she'd scoot over to Sydney's office, or try the courthouse for Rachel. Failing that, she could look up Bess at the television studio, or Alexi at his precinct. She could, she thought with a smile, all but trip over family, any direction she took.

The first thing she noticed inside the small, sunny gallery was Mikhail's work. Though the piece was new to her, she recognized his touch, and the subject, immediately. He'd carved his wife in polished mahogany. Madonna-like, Sydney held a baby in her arms. Their youngest, Freddie knew, Laurel. At Sydney's feet, three children of various ages and sizes sat. Walking closer, Freddie recognized her cousins, Griff, Moira and Adam. Unable to resist, she trailed a finger over the baby's cheek.

One day, she thought, she would hold her own child just that way. Hers and Nick's.

"I don't wait for faxes!" Mikhail shouted as he entered the gallery from a back room. "You wait for faxes! I have work!"

"But, Mik," came a plaintive voice from inside the room. "Washington said—"

"Do I care what Washington says? I don't think so. Tell them they can have three pieces, no more."

"But—"

"No more," he repeated, and closed the door behind him. He muttered to himself in Ukrainian as he crossed the gallery. Words, Freddie noted with a lifted brow, that she wasn't supposed to understand.

"Very artistic language, Uncle Mik."

He broke off in the middle of a very creative oath. "Freddie." With a hoot of laughter, he hoisted her off the ground as if she weighed no more than a favored rag doll. "Still just a peanut," he said, kissing her on the way down. "How's my pretty girl?"

"Excited to be here, and to see you."

He was, like his swearing, wild and exotic, with the golden eyes and raven hair of the Stanislaskis. Freddie had often thought that if she could paint, she would paint each member of her Ukrainian family in bold strokes and colors.

"I was just admiring your work," she told him. "It's incredibly beautiful."

"It's easy to create something beautiful when you have something beautiful to work with." He glanced toward the sculpture with love in his eyes. For the wood, Freddie reflected, but more, much more for the family he'd carved in it. "So, you've come to the big city to make your splash."

"I have indeed." With a flutter of lashes, Freddie hooked an arm through his and began to stroll, stopping here and there to admire a piece of art. "I'm hoping to work with Nick on the score he's beginning."

"Oh?" Mikhail quirked a brow. A man with so many women in his life understood their ways well, and appreciated them. "To write the words for his music?"

"Exactly. We'd make a good team, don't you think?"

"Yes, but it's not what I think, is it?" He smiled when her lips moved into a pout. "Our Nick, he can be stubborn, yes? And very hard of head. I can knock him in that head, if you like."

Her lips curved again before she laughed. "I hope it won't come to that, but I'll keep the offer in reserve." Her eyes changed, sharpened, and he could see clearly that she wasn't so much the child any longer. "I'm good, Uncle Mik. Music's in my blood, the way art's in yours."

"And when you see what you want..."

"I find a way to have it." Easily accepting her own arrogance, she shrugged her shoulders. That, too, was in the blood. "I want to work with Nick. I want to help him. And I'm going to."

"And from me you want...?"

"Family support for a chance to prove myself, if it becomes necessary, though I have an idea I can convince him without it." She tossed her hair back, in a gesture, Mikhail thought, very like his sister's. "What I do want, and need, is some advice about an apartment. I was hoping Aunt Sydney might have some ideas about a place near Lower the Boom."

"Maybe she does, but there's plenty of room with us. The children, you know how they would love to have you with them, and Sydney—" He caught her expression and sighed. "I promised your mama I would try. Natasha, she worries."

"She doesn't need to. She and Dad did a pretty good job of raising the self-reliant type. Just a small place, Uncle Mik," she continued quickly. "If you'd just ask Aunt Sydney to give me a call at the Waldorf. Maybe she and I can have lunch one day soon, if she's got time."

"She always has time for you. We all do."

"I know. And I intend to make a nuisance of myself. I want a place soon. Before," she added with a gleam in her eyes, "Grandma starts conspiring to have me move in with them in Brooklyn. I've got to go." She gave him a quick parting kiss. "I have another couple of stops to make." She darted for the door, paused. "Oh, and when you talk to Mama, tell her you tried."

With a wave, she was out on the street, and hailing another cab.

Now that her next seed was planted, Freddie had the cab take her to Lower the Boom, and wait as she went to the rear entrance to ring the security bell. Moments later, Nick's very sleepy and irritated voice barked through the intercom.

"Still in bed?" she said cheerfully. "You're getting too old for the wild life, Nicholas."

"Freddie? What the hell time is it?"

"Ten, but who's counting? Just buzz me in, will you? I've got something I want you to have. I'll just leave it on the table downstairs."

He swore, and she heard the sound of something crashing to the floor. "I'll come down."

"No, don't bother." She didn't think her system could handle facing him when he was half-awake and warm from bed. "I don't have time to visit, anyway. Just buzz me in, and call me later after you've gone over what I'm leaving for you."

"What is it?" he demanded as the buzzer sounded.

Instead of answering, Freddie hurried inside, dropped her music portfolio on Rio's table and raced out again. "Sorry to wake you, Nick," she called into the intercom. "If you're free tonight, we'll have dinner. See you."

"Wait a damn—"

But she was already dashing toward the front of the building and her waiting cab. She sat back, let out a long breath and closed her eyes. If he didn't want her—her talents, she corrected—after he went through what she'd left for him, she was back to ground zero.

Think positive, she ordered herself. Straightening, she folded her arms. "Take me to Saks," she told the driver.

When a woman had a potential date with the man she intended to marry, the very least she deserved was a new dress.

Chapter Two

By the time Nick found and dragged on a pair of jeans and stumbled downstairs, Freddie was long gone. He had nothing to curse but the air as he rapped his bare toe against the thick leg of the kitchen table. Hopping, he scowled at the slim leather portfolio she'd left behind.

What the hell was the kid up to? he wondered. Waking him up at dawn, leaving mystery packages in the kitchen. Still grumbling, he snatched up the portfolio and headed back up to his apartment. He needed coffee.

To get into his own kitchen, he expertly stepped over and maneuvered around discarded newspapers, clothing, abandoned sheets of music. He tossed Freddie's portfolio on the cluttered counter and coaxed his brain to remember the basic functions of his coffeemaker.

He wasn't a morning person.

Once the pot was making a hopeful hiss, he opened the refrigerator and eyed the contents blearily. Breakfast was not on the menu at Lower the Boom and was the only meal he couldn't con out of Rio, so his choices were limited. The minute he sniffed the remains of a carton of milk and gagged, he knew cold cereal was out. He opted for a candy bar instead.

Fortified with two sources of caffeine, he sat down, lighted a cigarette, then unzipped the portfolio.

He was set to resent whatever it was that Freddie had considered important enough to wake him up for. Even small-town rich kids should know that bars didn't close until late. And since he'd taken over the late shift from his brother, Nick rarely found his bed before three.

With a huge yawn, he dumped the contents of the portfolio out. Neatly printed sheet music spilled onto the table.

Figures, he thought. The kid had the idea stuck in her head that they were going to work together. And he knew Freddie well enough to understand that when she had something lodged in her brain, it took a major crowbar to pry it loose.

Sure, she had talent, he mused. He would hardly expect the daughter of Spencer Kimball to be tone-deaf. But he didn't much care for partnerships in the first place. True, he'd worked well enough with Lorrey on *Last Stop*. But Lorrey wasn't a relative. And he didn't smell like candy-coated sin.

Block that thought, LeBeck, he warned himself, and dragged back his disordered hair before he picked up the first sheet that came to hand. The least he could do for his little cousin was give her work a look.

And when he did, his brows drew together. The music was his own. Something he'd half finished, fiddled with on one of the family visits to West Virginia. He could remember now sitting at the piano in the music room of the big stone house, Freddie on the bench beside him. Last summer? he wondered. The summer before? Not so long ago he couldn't recall that she'd been grown up, and that he'd had a little trouble whenever she leaned into him, or shot him one of those looks with those incredibly big gray eyes.

Nick shook his head, rubbed his face and concentrated on the music again. She'd polished it up, he noted, and frowned a bit over the idea of someone fooling with his work. And she'd added lyrics, romantic love-story words that suited the mood of the music.

"It Was Ever You," she'd titled it. As the tune began to play in his head, he gathered up all the sheets and left his half-finished breakfast for the piano in the living room.

Ten minutes later, he was on the phone to the Waldorf and leaving the first of several messages for Miss Frederica Kimball.

* * *

It was late afternoon before Freddie returned to her suite, flushed with pleasure and laden with purchases. In her opinion, she'd spent the most satisfying of days, shopping, lunching with Rachel and Bess, then shopping some more. After dumping her bags in the parlor, she headed for the phone. At this time of day, she thought, she could catch some, if not all, of her family at home. The blinking message light caught her eye, but before she could lift the receiver, the phone rang.

"Hello."

"Damn it, Fred, where have you been all day?"

Her lips curved at the sound of Nick's voice. "Hi there. Up and around, are you?"

"Real cute, Fred. I've been trying to get hold of you all day. I was about to call Alex and have him put out an APB." He'd pictured her mugged, assaulted, kidnapped.

She balanced on one foot, toeing off her shoes. "Well, if you had, he'd have told you I spent part of the day having lunch with his wife. Is there a problem?"

"Problem? No, no, why would there be a problem?" Even through the phone, sarcasm dripped. "You wake me up at the crack of dawn—"

"After ten," she corrected.

"And then you run off for hours," he continued, ignoring her. "I seem to recall you yelling something about wanting me to call you."

"Yes." She braced herself, grateful he couldn't see her, or the hope in her eyes. "Did you have a chance to look at the music I left for you?"

He opened his mouth, settled back again and played it cool. "I gave it a look." He'd spent hours reading it, poring over it, playing it. "It's not bad—especially the parts that are mine."

Even though he couldn't see her, her chin shot up. "It's a lot better than not bad—especially the parts that I polished." The gleam in her eyes was pure pride now. "How about the lyrics?"

They ranged from the poetic to the wickedly wry, and had impressed him more than he wanted to admit to either of them. "You've got a nice touch, Fred."

"Oh, be still my heart."

"They're good, okay?" He released a long breath. "I don't know what you want me to do about it, but—"

"Why don't we talk about that? Are you free tonight?"

He contemplated the date he had lined up, thought of the music, and dismissed everything else. "There's nothing I can't get out of."

Her brow lifted. Work, she wondered, or a woman? "Fine. I'll buy you dinner. Come by the hotel about seven-thirty."

"Look, why don't we just—"

"We both have to eat, don't we? Wear a suit, and we'll make it an event. Seven-thirty." With her bottom lip caught in her teeth, she hung up before he could argue.

Jittery, she lowered herself to perch on the arm of the chair. It was working, she assured herself, just as she'd planned. There was no reason to be nervous. Right, she thought, rolling her eyes, no reason at all.

She was about to begin the courtship and seduction of the man she'd loved nearly her entire life. And if it went wrong, she'd have a broken heart, suffer total humiliation and have all her hopes and dreams shattered.

No reason to panic.

To give herself a boost, she picked up the phone again and called West Virginia. The familiar voice that answered smoothed out all the rough edges and made her smile.

"Mama."

At seven-thirty, Nick was pacing the lobby of the Waldorf. He was not happy to be there. He hated wearing a suit. He hated fancy restaurants and the pretentious service they fostered. If Freddie had given him half a chance, he would have insisted she come by the bar, where they could talk in peace.

It was true that since he'd found success on Broadway, he was occasionally called upon to socialize, even attend functions that required formal wear. But he didn't have to like it. He still just wanted what he'd always wanted—to be able to write and play his music without hassles.

Nick outstared one of the uniformed bellmen, who obviously thought he was a suspicious character.

Damn right I am, Nick thought with some humor. Zack and Rachel and the rest of the Stanislaskis might have saved him from prison and the prospect of a lifetime on the shady side of the law, but there was still a core of the rebellious, lonely boy inside him.

His stepbrother, Zack, had bought him his first piano over a decade before, and Nick could still remember the total shock and wonder he'd felt that someone, anyone, had cared enough to understand and respond to his unspoken dreams. No, he'd never forgotten, and to his mind, he'd never fully paid back the debt he owed the brother who had stuck by him through the very worst of times.

And he'd changed, sure. He no longer looked for trouble. It was vital to him to do nothing to shame the family who had accepted him and welcomed him into their midst. But he was still Nick LeBeck, former petty thief, con artist and hustler, the kid who'd first met former public defender Rachel Stanislaski on the wrong side of prison bars.

Wearing a suit only put a thin layer between then and now.

He tugged on his tie, detesting it. He didn't think back very often. There was no need. Something about Freddie was making him switch back and forth between past and present.

The first time he saw her, she'd been about thirteen, a little china doll. Cute, sweet, harmless. And he loved her. Of course he did. In a purely familial way. The fact that she'd grown into a woman didn't change that. He was still six years older, her more experienced cousin.

But the woman who stepped out of the elevator didn't look like anyone's cousin.

What the hell had she done to herself? Nick jammed his hands in his pockets and scowled at her as she crossed the lobby in a short, snug little dress the color of just-ripened apricots. She'd clipped up her hair, and it showed entirely too much of slender neck and smooth shoulders. Glittery colored gems swung from her ears, and one tear-shaped sapphire nestled comfortably between the curve of her breasts.

The kind of female trick, Nick knew, that drew a man's eyes to that tempting point and made his fingers itch.

Not that his did, he assured himself, and kept them safely in his pockets.

Her dimples flashed as she spotted him, and he concentrated on them, rather than on her legs as she walked to him.

"Hi. I hope you haven't been waiting long." She rose on her toes to kiss him at the left corner of his mouth. "You look wonderful."

"I don't see why we had to get all dressed up to eat."

"So I could wear the outfit I bought today." She turned a saucy circle, laughing. "Like it?"

He was lucky his tongue wasn't hanging out. "It's fine. What there is of it. You're going to get cold."

To her credit, she didn't snarl at the brotherly opinion of her appearance. "I don't think so. The car's waiting just outside." She took his hand, linking fingers with him as they walked out of the lobby toward the sleek black limo at the curb.

"You got a limo? To go to dinner?"

"I felt like indulging myself." With the ease of long practice, she flashed a smile at the driver before sliding smoothly into the car. "You're my first date in New York."

It was said casually, as if she expected to have many more dates, with many more men. Nick only grunted as he climbed in after her.

"I'll never understand rich people."

"You're not exactly on poverty row these days, Nick," she reminded him. "A Broadway hit going into its second year, a Tony nomination, another musical to be scored."

He moved his shoulders, still uncomfortable with the idea of true monetary success. "I don't hang around in limos."

"So enjoy." She settled back, feeling a great deal like Cinderella on her way to the ball. The big difference was, she was going there with her Prince Charming. "Big Sunday dinner at Grandma's coming up," she said.

"Yeah, I got the word on it."

"I can't wait to see them, and all the kids. I dropped by Uncle Mik's gallery this morning. Have you seen the piece he did on Aunt Sydney and the children?"

"Yeah." Nick's eyes softened. He almost forgot he was wearing a suit and riding in a limo. "It's beautiful. The baby's terrific. She's got this way of climbing up your leg and into your lap. Bess is having another one, you know."

"So she told me at lunch. There's no stopping

those Ukrainians. Papa's going to have to start buying those gumdrops he likes to pass out by the gross.''

''You don't worry about teeth,'' Nick said in Yuri's thick accent. ''All my grandbabies have teeth like iron.''

Freddie laughed, shifting so that her knee brushed his. ''They have a wedding anniversary coming up.''

''Next month, right.''

''We were kicking around ideas for a party at lunch. We thought about hiring a hall, or a hotel ballroom, but we all thought it would be more fun, and more true to them, if we kept it simpler. Would you and Zack hold it in the bar?''

''Sure, that's no problem. Hell of a lot more fun there than at some ritzy ballroom.'' And he wouldn't have to wear a damned suit. ''Rio can handle the food.''

''You and I can handle the music.''

He shot her a cautious look. ''Yeah, we could do that.''

''And we thought we could do a group present. Did you know Grandma's always wanted to go to Paris?''

''Nadia, Paris?'' He smiled at the thought. ''No. How do you know?''

''It was something she said to Mama, not too long ago. She didn't say too much—you know she wouldn't. Just how she'd always wondered if it was as romantic as all the songs claimed. Oh, and a couple of other things. So we were thinking, if we could give them a trip, fly them over there for a couple of weeks, get them a suite at the Ritz or something.''

"It's a great idea. Yuri and Nadia do Paris.'' He was still grinning over it when the limo glided to the curb.

"Where have you always wanted to go?''

"Hmm?'' Nick climbed out, automatically offering a hand to assist her. "Oh, I don't know. The best place I've ever been is New Orleans. Incredible music. You can stand on any street corner and be blown away by it. The Caribbean's not bad either. Remember when Zack and Rachel and I sailed down there? God, that was before any of the kids came along.''

"You sent me a postcard from Saint Martin,'' she murmured. She still had it.

"It was the first time I'd been anywhere. Zack decided that as a crew member my best contribution was as ballast, so I ended up doing mostly kitchen duty. I bitched all the way and loved every minute of it.''

They stepped inside, out of the slight spring chill and into the warmth and muted light of the restaurant. "Kimball,'' Freddie told the maître d', and found herself well satisfied when they were led to a quiet corner booth.

Very close to perfect, she thought, with candles flickering in silver holders on the white linen tablecloth, the scent of good food, the gleam of fine crystal. Nick might not realize he was being courted, but she thought she was doing an excellent job of it.

"Should we have some wine?'' she asked.

"Sure." He took the leather-bound list. His years of working a bar had taught him something about choosing the right vintage. He skimmed the list and shook his head over the ridiculous price markups. Well, it was Fred's party.

"The Sancerre, '88," he told the hovering sommelier. It was a profession, Nick had always thought, that made a guy look as though he had an ashtray hanging around his neck.

"Yes, sir. Excellent choice."

"I figure it should be, since it's marked up about three hundred percent." While Freddie struggled with a laugh and the sommelier struggled with his dignity, Nick passed the list back and lighted a cigarette. "So, any luck on finding an apartment?"

"I didn't do a lot about it today, but I think Sydney will come up with something."

"Finding one in New York isn't a snap, kid. And you can get conned. There are plenty of people out there just waiting for a chance to gobble up fresh meat. You ought to think about moving in with one of the family for the time being."

She arched a brow. "Want a roommate?"

He gaped at her, blinked, then blew out smoke. "That wasn't what I meant."

"Actually, being roomies would be handy once we start working together—"

"Hold it. You're getting ahead of yourself."

"Am I?" With a slight smile, she sat back as the sommelier presented the wine label for Nick's inspection.

"Fine," he said with an impatient wave of his

hand, but there was no getting rid of the man until the ritual of the wine was completed. Nick handed the cork to Freddie. Cork smelled like cork, and he'd be damned if he'd sniff it. To speed the business up, he took a quick sip of the sample that was poured into his glass. "Great, let's have it."

With strained dignity, the sommelier poured Freddie's wine, then topped off Nick's, before nestling the bottle into the waiting silver bucket.

"Now listen—" Nick began.

"It *was* an excellent choice," Freddie mused as she savored the first sip. Dry, and nicely light. "You know, I trust your taste in certain areas, Nicholas, without reservation. This is one of them," she said, lifting her glass. "And music's another. You may be reluctant to admit that your little Freddie's as good as you are, but your musical integrity won't let you do otherwise."

"Nobody's saying you're as good as I am, kid. But you're not bad." Giving in, just a little, he tapped his glass against hers. For a moment, he lost his train of thought. Something about the way the candlelight played in those smoky eyes. And the look in them, as if she had a secret she wasn't quite ready to share with him. "Anyhow." He cleared his throat, brought himself back. "I liked your stuff."

"Oh, Mr. LeBeck." She lowered her lashes, fluttered them. "I don't know what to say."

"You've always got plenty to say. The one number—'It Was Ever You'? It may fit in with the score."

"I thought it would." She smiled at his narrowed

eyes. "As the daughter of Spencer Kimball, I do have certain connections. I've read the book, Nick. It's wonderful. The story manages to be beautifully old-fashioned and contemporary at the same time. It has a terrific central love story, wit, comedy. And with Maddy O'Hurley in the lead—"

"How do you know that?"

She smiled again, and couldn't prevent it from leaning toward smug. "Connections. My father's done quite a bit of work for her husband. Reed Valentine's an old friend of the family."

"Connections," Nick muttered. "Why do you need me? You could go straight to Valentine. He's backing the play."

"I could." Unconcerned with the tone of annoyance, Freddie pursed her lips and studied her wine. "But that's not the way I want to do it." She lifted her gaze, met his, held it. "I want you to want me, Nick. If you don't, it wouldn't work between us." She waited a beat. Could he see that she wasn't simply talking about music, but about her life, as well? Their life. "I'll do everything I can to convince you that you do want me. Then, if you can look at me and tell me you don't, I'll live with it."

Something was stirring deep in his gut. Something skittish and dangerous and unwanted. He had an urge, a shockingly strong one, to reach out and run his fingers down that smooth ivory-and-rose cheek. Instead, he took a careful breath and crushed out his cigarette.

"Okay, Fred, convince me."

The hideous tightness around her heart loosened. "I will," she said, "but let's order dinner first."

She chose her meal almost at random. Her mind was too busy formulating what she should say, and how she should say it, to worry about something as insignificant as food. She sipped her wine, watching Nick as he completed his part of the order. When he finished and looked back over at her, she was smiling.

"What?"

"I was just thinking." Reaching over, she laid a hand over his. "About the first time I saw you. You walked into that wonderful chaos at Grandma's and looked as if you'd been hit by a brick."

He smiled back at her, on easy ground again. "I'd never seen anything like it. I never believed people lived that way—all that yelling and laughing, kids running around, food everywhere."

"And Katie marched right up to you and demanded you pick her up."

"Your little sister's always had her eye on me."

"So have I."

He started to laugh, then discovered it wasn't all that funny. "Come on."

"Really. One look at you, and my in-the-middle-of-puberty-hell heart started beating against my ribs. Your hair was a little longer than it is now, a little lighter. You were wearing an earring."

With a half laugh, he rubbed his earlobe. "Haven't done that in a while."

"I thought you were beautiful, exotic, just like the rest of them."

Initial embarrassment at her description turned to puzzlement. "The rest of who?"

"The family. God, those wonderful Ukrainian Gypsy looks, my father's aristocratic handsomeness, Sydney's impeccable glamor, Zack, the tough weather-beaten hunk."

He'd like that one, Nick thought with a grin.

"Then you, somewhere between rock star and James Dean." She sighed, exaggerating the sound. "I was a goner. Every girl's entitled to a memorable first crush. And you were certainly mine."

"Well." He wasn't sure how to react. "I guess I'm flattered."

"You should be. I gave up Bobby MacAroy and Harrison Ford for you."

"Harrison Ford? Pretty impressive." He relaxed as their appetizers were served. "But who the hell's Bobby MacAroy?"

"Only the cutest boy in my eighth-grade class. Of course, he was unaware that I planned for us to get married and have five kids." She lifted her shoulder, let it fall.

"His loss."

"You bet. Anyway, that day I just sort of looked at you, and worked on working up the courage to actually speak. Little freckled Fred," she mused. "Among all those exotic birds."

"You were like porcelain," he murmured. "A little blond doll with enormous eyes. I remember saying something about how you didn't look like your little brother and sister, and you explained that Natasha was technically your stepmother. I felt sorry for you.'' He looked up again, losing himself for a moment in those depthless eyes. ''Because I felt sorry for me—the out-of-step stepbrother. And you sat there, so serious, and told me *step* was just a word. It hit me,'' he told her. ''It really hit for the first time. And it made a difference.''

Her eyes had gone moist and soft. ''I never knew that. You seemed so easy with Zack.''

''I tried to hate him for a long time. Never quite pulled it off, though I worked pretty hard at making life miserable for both of us. And then, I was hung up on Rachel.''

''Hung up? But...'' Diplomatically Freddie trailed off and took an avid interest in her food.

He was easy with the memory now, had been for years. ''Yeah, I was barely nineteen. And because I figured she was a class act with a great figure and incredible legs, I didn't see how she could resist me. You're blushing, Fred.

''Hey, every boy's entitled to one memorable crush.'' He grinned at her. ''I was pretty ticked when I figured out Rachel and Zack had a thing going, made an idiot out of myself. Then I got over it, because they had something special. And because it finally occurred to me that I loved her, but I wasn't *in* love with her. That's how crushes end, right?''

She eyed him levelly. ''Sometimes. And in a roundabout way, what we've been talking about right here proves my point about why we should work together.''

He waited while their appetizers were cleared and the second course was served. Interested, he picked up the wineglass that had just been topped off again. "How?"

To add emphasis to her pitch, Freddie leaned forward. And her perfume drifted over him so that his mouth watered. "We're connected, Nick. On a lot of levels. We have a history, and some similarities in that history that go back to before we met."

"You're losing me."

She gave an impatient shake of her head. "We don't have to get into that. I know you, Nicholas. Better than you may think. I know what your music means to you. Salvation."

His eyes clouded, and he lost interest in his meal. "That's pretty strong."

"It's absolutely accurate," she corrected. "Success is a by-product. It's the music that matters. You'd write it for nothing, you'd play it for nothing. It's what kept you from sinking without a trace, every bit as much as the family did. You need it, and you need me to write the words for it. Because I hear the words, Nick, when I hear your music. I hear what you want it to say, because I understand you. And because I love you."

He studied her, trying to separate emotion and practicality. But she was right. He'd never been able to separate the two with his music. The emotion came first, and she'd tapped into that with the words she'd already written, and with the words she'd just spoken.

"You make a strong case for yourself, Fred."

"For us. We'll make a hell of a team, Nick. So

much stronger and better than either of us could be separately."

The music he'd played that morning wound through his head, her lyrics humming with it. *It was ever you, in my heart, in my mind. No one before and no one after. For only one face have I always pined. You are the tears and the laughter.*

A lonely song, he thought, and an achingly hopeful one. She was right, he decided—it was exactly what he'd intended.

"Let's play it like this, Freddie. We'll take some time, see how it goes. If we can come up with two other solid songs for the libretto, we'll take it to the producers."

Under the table, she tapped her nervous fingers on her knee. "And if they approve the material?"

"If they approve the material, you've got yourself a partner." He lifted his glass. "Deal?"

"Oh, yes." She tapped her glass against his, sounding a celebratory note. "It's a deal."

It was far more than the wine that had her feeling giddy when Nick walked her up to her hotel room after dinner. Laughing, she whirled, pressing her back against the door and beaming at him. "We're going to be fabulous together. I know it."

He tucked stray curls behind her ear, barely noticing that his fingertip skimmed the lobe, lingered. "We'll see how it flies. Tomorrow, my place, my piano. Bring food."

"All right. I'll be there first thing in the morning."

"You come before noon, I'll have to kill you. Where's your key, kid?"

"Right here." She waved it under his nose before sliding it into the slot. "Want to come in?"

"I've got to finish off the late shift and close the bar. So..." His words, and his thoughts, trailed off as she turned back and slipped her arms around him. The quick flash of heat stunned him. "Get some sleep," he began, and lowered his head to give her a chaste peck on the cheek.

She wasn't that giddy—or perhaps she was just giddy enough. She shifted, tilting her face so that their lips met. Only for two heartbeats, two long, unsteady heartbeats.

She savored it, the taste of him, the firm, smooth texture of his mouth, and the quick, instinctive tightening of his hands on her shoulders.

Then she drew away, a bright, determined smile on her lips that gave no clue as to her own rocky pulse. "Good night, Nicholas."

He didn't move, not a single muscle, even after she shut the door in his face. It was the sound of his own breath whooshing out that broke the spell. He turned, walked slowly toward the elevators.

His cousin, he reminded himself. She was his cousin, not some sexy little number he could enjoy temporarily. He lifted a hand to push the button for the lobby, noticed it wasn't quite steady, and cursed under his breath.

Cousins, he thought again. Who had a family history and a potential working relationship. No way he was going to forget that. No way in hell.

Chapter Three

"Hi, Rio." Freddie balanced bag, purse and briefcase as she entered through the kitchen of Lower the Boom.

"Hey, little doll." Busy with lunch preparations, Rio had both hands occupied himself. "What's doing?"

"Nick and I are working together today," she told him as she headed for the stairs.

"Be lucky if you don't have to pull him out of bed by his hair."

She only chuckled and kept going. "He said noon. It's noon." On the dot, she added to herself, maneuvering up the narrow, curved staircase. She gave the door at the top a sharp rap, waited. Tapped her foot. Shifted her bags. Okay, Nicholas, she thought, up and at 'em. After fighting the door open, she gave a warning shout.

In the silence that followed, she heard the faint sound of water running. In the shower, she decided, and, satisfied, carried her bundles into the kitchen.

She'd taken him seriously when he told her to bring food. Out of the bag she took deli cartons of potato salad, pasta salad, pickles and waxed-paper-wrapped sandwiches. After setting them out, she went on a search for cold drinks.

It didn't take long for her to realize they had a choice between beer and flat seltzer. And that Nick's kitchen was crying out for a large dose of industrial-strength cleaner.

When he came in a few minutes later, the sleeves of her sweater were pushed up and she was up to her elbows in steaming, soapy water.

"What's going on?"

"This place is a disgrace," she said without turning around. "You should be ashamed of yourself, living like this. I wrapped the medical experiments that were in the fridge in that plastic bag. I'd take them out and bury them if I were you."

He grunted and headed for the coffeepot.

"When's the last time you took a mop to this floor?"

"I think it was September 1990." He yawned and, trying to adjust his eyes to morning, measured out coffee. "Did you bring food?"

"On the table."

With a frown he studied the salads, the sandwiches. "Where's breakfast?"

"It's lunchtime," she said between her teeth.

"Time's relative, Fred." Experimentally, he bit into a pickle.

With a clatter, Freddie set the last of the dishes she'd found crusted in the sink aside to drain. "The least you could do is go in and pick up some of the mess in the living room. I don't know how you expect to work in this place."

The tart taste of the pickle improved his spirits, so he took another bite. "I pick it up the third Sunday of every month, whether it needs it or not."

She turned, fisted her hands on her hips. "Well, pick it up now. I'm not working in this pit, clothes everywhere, trash, dust an inch thick."

Leaning back on the table, he grinned at her. Her hair was pulled back, in an attempt to tame it that failed beautifully. Her eyes were stormy, her mouth was set. She looked, he thought, like an insulted fairy.

"God, you're cute, Fred."

Now those stormy eyes narrowed. "You know I hate that."

"Yeah." His grin only widened.

With dignity, she ripped off a paper towel from a roll on the counter to dry her hands. "What are you staring at?"

"You. I'm waiting for you to pout. You're even cuter when you pout."

She would not, she promised herself, be amused. "You're really pushing it, Nick."

"It stopped you from ordering me around, the way you do with Brandon."

"I do not order my brother around."

Nick scooted around her to get one of the coffee mugs she'd just washed. "Sure you do. Face it, kid, you're bossy."

"I certainly am not."

"Bossy, spoiled, and cute as a little button."

To prove her own control, she took one long, deep breath. "I'm going to hit you in a minute."

"That's a good one," Nick acknowledged as he poured coffee. "Sticking your chin up. It's almost as good as a pout."

For lack of something better, she tossed the balled paper towel so that it bounced off his head. "I came here to work, not to be insulted. If this is the best you can do, I'll just go."

He was chuckling as she started to storm by him. For the first time since she'd come to New York, he felt their relationship was back on the level where it belonged. Big-brotherly cousin to pip-squeak. He was chuckling still as he grabbed her arm and whirled her around.

"Ah, come on, Fred, don't go away mad."

"I'm not mad," she said, even as her elbow jabbed into his stomach.

His breath whooshed out on a laugh. "You can do better than that. You've got to put your body behind it, if you want results."

Challenged, she attempted to, and the quick tussle threw them both off balance. He was laughing as they fought for balance, as she ended up with her back against the refrigerator, his hands at her hips, hers gripping his forearms.

Then he stopped laughing, when he realized he was pressed against her. And she was so soft and small. Her eyes fired up at him. And they were so wide and deep. Her mouth, pouting now, drew his gaze down. And it was so deliciously full.

She felt the change slowly, a melting of her body, a thrumming in her blood. This was what she had been waiting for, yearning for—the man-to-woman embrace, the awareness that was like light bursting in the head. Following instinct, she slid her hands up his arms to his shoulders.

He would have kissed her, he realized as he jerked back. And it would have had nothing to do with family affection. In another instant, he would have kissed her the way a hungry man kisses a willing woman—and broken more than a decade of trust.

"Nick." She said it quietly, with the plea just a whisper in the word.

He'd scared her, he thought, berating himself, and lifted his hands, palms out. "Sorry. I shouldn't have teased you like that." More comfortable with distance, he backed up until he could reach the mug he'd set on the table.

"It's all right." She managed a smile as the warmth that had shuddered into her system drained out again. "I'm used to it. But I still want you to pick up that mess."

His lips curved in response. It was going to be all right after all. "My place, my mess, my piano. You'll have to get used to it."

She debated a moment, then nodded. "Fine. And

when I get my place, and my piano, we'll work there.''

''Maybe.'' He got a fork and began to eat potato salad out of the carton. ''Why don't you get some coffee, and we'll talk about what I'm after with the score?''

''What *we're* after,'' she corrected. She plucked a mug out of the drain. ''Partner.''

They sat in the kitchen for an hour, discussing, dissecting and debating the theme and heart of the score for *First, Last and Always*. The musical was to span ten years, taking the leads from a youthful infatuation into a hasty marriage and hastier divorce and ultimately to a mature, fulfilled relationship.

Happy ever after, Freddie called it.

The perpetual rocky road, was Nick's opinion.

They both agreed that the two viewpoints would add zest to the work, and punch to the music.

''She loves him,'' Freddie said as they settled at the piano. ''The first time she sees him.''

''She's in love with love.'' Nick set up the tape recorder. ''They both are. They're young and stupid. That's one of the things that makes the characters appealing, funny and real.''

''Hmmm.''

''Listen.'' He took his place on the piano bench beside her, hip to hip with her. ''It opens with the crowd scene. Lots of movement, lights, speed. Everybody's in a hurry.''

He flipped through his staff sheets and, with what

Freddie decided was some sort of inner radar, unerringly chose the one he wanted.

"So I want to hit the audience with the confusion and rush." He adjusted the synthesizer keyboard on the stand beside him. "And that energy of youth in the opening number."

"When they run into each other, literally."

"Right. Here."

He started to play, a jarring opening note that would wake the senses. Freddie closed her eyes and let the music flood over her.

Quick, full, sometimes clashing notes. Oh, yes, she could see what he wanted. Impatience. Self-absorption. Hurry up, get out of my way. In part of her mind, she could see the stage, packed with dancers, convoluted choreography, the noise from traffic. Horns blaring.

"Needs more brass here," Nick muttered. He'd all but forgotten Freddie's presence as he stopped to make notes and fiddle with the synthesizer.

"'Don't Stop Now.'"

"I just want to punch up the brass."

She only shook her head at him and placed her own hands on the piano keys. With her eyes narrowed on the notes he'd scribbled on the staff paper, she began, voice melding with music.

"'Don't stop now. I've got places to go, people to see. Don't know how I'm supposed to put up with anybody but me.'"

Her voice was pure. Funny, he'd almost forgotten that. Low, smooth, easily confident. Surprisingly sexy.

"You're quick," he murmured.

"I'm good." She continued to play while words and movement ran through her head. "It should be a chorus number, lots of voices, point and counterpoint, with an overlying duet between the principals. He's going one way, she the other. The words should overlap and blend, overlap and blend."

"Yeah." He picked up the fill on the synthesizer, playing with her. "That's the idea."

She slanted him a look, a smug smile. "I know."

It took them more than three hours and two pots of coffee to hammer out the basics of the opening. Not wanting to jar her system with any more of the caffeine Nick seemed to thrive on, Freddie insisted he go down to the bar and find her some club soda. Alone, she made a few minute changes to both words and music on the staff sheet. Even as she began to try them out, the phone interrupted her.

Humming the emerging song in her head, she rose to answer.

"Hello?"

"Why, hi. Is Nick around?"

The slow, sultry, southern female voice had Freddie lifting a brow. "He'll be back in just a second. He had to run down to the bar."

"Oh, well, I'll just hang on then, if it's all right with you. I'm Lorelie."

I bet you are, Freddie thought grimly. "Hello, Lorelie, I'm Fred."

"Not Nick's little cousin Fred?"

"That's me," she said between her teeth. "Little cousin Fred."

"Well, I'm just thrilled to talk to you, honey." Warmed, honeyed molasses all but seeped through the phone line. "Nick told me he was visiting with you last night. I didn't mind postponing our date, seeing as it was family."

Damn it, she'd known it was a woman. "That's very understanding of you, Lorelie."

"Oh, now, a young girl like you, alone in New York, needs the men in her family to look out for her. I've been here myself five years, and I'm still not used to all the people. And everybody just moves so fast."

"Some aren't as fast as others," Freddie muttered. "Where are you from, Lorelie?" she asked, politely, she hoped.

"Atlanta, honey. Born and bred. But up here with these Yankees is where the modeling and television work is."

"You're a model?" Didn't it just figure?

"That's right, but I've been doing a lot more television commercials these days. It just wipes you out, if you know what I mean."

"I'm sure it does."

"That's how I met Nick. I just dropped into the bar one afternoon, after the longest shoot. I asked him to fix me a long cool something. And he said I looked like a long cool something to him." Lorelie's laugh was a silver tinkle that set Freddie's teeth on edge. "Isn't Nick the sweetest thing?"

Freddie glanced up as the sweetest thing came

back in with an armload of soda bottles. "Oh, he certainly is. We're always saying that about him."

"Well, I think it's just fine that Nick would tend to his little cousin on her first trip alone to the big city. You're a southern girl, too, aren't you, honey?"

"Well, south of the Mason-Dixon line, at least, Lorelie. We're practically sisters. Here's our sweet Nick now."

Face dangerously bland, Freddie held out the receiver. "Your magnolia blossom's on the phone."

He set the bottles down in the most convenient place, on the floor, then took the phone. "Lorelie?" With one wary eye on Freddie, he listened. "Yeah, she is. No, it's West Virginia. Yeah, close enough. Ah, listen..." He turned his back, lowering his voice as Freddie began to noodle softly at the piano. "I'm working right now. No, no, tonight's fine. Come by the bar about seven." He cleared his throat, wondering why he felt so uncomfortable. "I'm looking forward to that, too. Oh, really?" He glanced cautiously over his shoulder at Freddie. "That sounds... interesting. See you tonight."

After he hung up, he bent down to retrieve one of the bottles. As he unscrewed the top and took it to Freddie, he wondered why it should feel like a pathetic peace offering. "It's cold."

"Thanks."

And so, he noted, was her voice. Ice-cold.

She took the bottle, tipped it back for a long sip. "Should I apologize for taking you away from Lorelie last night?"

"No. We're not— She's just— No."

"It's so flattering that you told her all about your little lost cousin from West Virginia." Freddie set the bottle down and let her fingers flow over the keys. Better there than curled around Nick's throat. "I can't believe she bought such a pathetic cliché."

"I just told her the truth." He stood, scowling and feeling very put-upon.

"That I needed to be looked after?"

"I didn't say that, exactly. Look, what's the big deal? You wanted to have dinner, and I rearranged my plans."

"Next time, just tell me you have a date, Nick. I won't have any trouble making plans of my own." Incensed, she pushed away from the piano and began stuffing her papers into her briefcase. "And I am not your little cousin, and I don't need to be looked after or tended to. Anybody but a total jerk could see that I'm a grown woman, well able to take care of herself."

"I never said you weren't—"

"You say it every time you look at me." She kicked a pile of clothes away as she stormed across the room for her purse. "It so happens that there are a few men around who would be more than happy to have dinner with me without considering it a duty."

"Hold on."

"I will not hold on." She whirled back, curls flying around her face. "You'd better take a good look, Nicholas LeBeck. I am not little Freddie anymore, and I won't be treated like some family pet who needs a pat on the head.''

Baffled, he dragged his hands through his hair. ''What the hell's gotten into you?''

''Nothing!'' She shouted it, frustrated beyond control. ''Nothing, you idiot. Go cuddle up with your southern comfort.''

When she slammed the door, Nick leaned down to open a club soda for himself. He could only shake his head. To think, he mused, she'd been such a sweet-tempered kid.

Freddie worked off a great deal of her anger with a long walk. When she felt she was calm enough to speak without spewing broken glass, she stopped at a phone booth and checked in with Sydney. The conversation did quite a bit to lift her spirits.

Afterward, armed with an address, she rushed off to view a vacant one-bedroom apartment three blocks from Nick's.

It was perfect. While Freddie wandered from room to room, she envisioned the furnishings she'd place here, the rugs she'd place there. Her own home, she thought, with room enough for a piano under the window, space enough for a pullout sofa so that her brother or sister could come and stay for visits.

And best of all, close enough that she could keep an eye on Nick.

How do you like that, Nicholas? she wondered as she grinned at her view of Manhattan. I'm going to be looking out for you. I love you so much, you stupid jerk.

Sighing, she turned away from the window and walked into the kitchen. It was small and needed some paint to perk it up, but she would see to that. She'd enjoy choosing the right cookware, the pots and pans and kitchen implements. She loved to cook, and even as a child had loved the big kitchen in her home in West Virginia, the wonderfully crowded kitchen at her grandmother's in Brooklyn.

She'd cook for Nick here, she thought, running a finger over the smooth butcher-block countertop, if he played his cards right. No. She smiled at herself, and at her own impatience. It was she who had to play the cards, and play them right.

She'd been too hard on him, even if he had been a jerk. She'd spent more than half her life in love with him, but he spent that same amount of time thinking of her as a little cousin—if not by blood, then by circumstance. It was going to take more than one romantic dinner and one afternoon as colleagues to change that.

And change it she would. Hands on hips, she began another tour of the apartment. Just as she would build a life here, one that reflected her own taste and grew from the solid, loving background she'd been blessed with. And before she was done, the world she created would be filled with music and color and love.

And, by God, with Nick.

It was nearly seven when Nick came down to the bar. Zack lifted a brow as he mixed a stinger. ''Hot date?''

"Lorelie."

"Oh, yeah." Now Zack wiggled his brows. "Tall, willowy brunette with rose petals in her voice."

"That's the one." Nick moved behind the bar to help fill orders. "We're just going to catch some dinner. Then we'll come back here so I can relieve you."

"I can cover for you."

"No, it's no problem. She likes hanging out here. After I close up, we'll figure out something else to do."

"I bet you will. Table six needs two drafts and a bourbon and branch."

"Got it."

"Hey, did you hear about Freddie's apartment."

Nick's hand paused on the lever. "What apartment?"

"Found one just a couple blocks from here. She's already signed the papers." Zack filled an empty bowl with beer nuts. "You just missed her. She came in to celebrate."

"Did anybody look over the place for her? Mik?"

"She didn't say. Kid's got a good head on her shoulders."

"Yeah. I guess. She should have gotten Rachel to look over the lease, though."

Chuckling, Zack laid a hand on Nick's shoulder as he was finishing preparing the order. "Hey, the little birds have to leave the nest sometime."

With a shrug, Nick placed the drinks on the end

of the bar for the waitress. "So, she went on back to the hotel?"

"Nope. Went out with Ben."

"Ben." Nick's fingers froze on the cloth he'd picked up to wipe the bar. "What do you mean, she went out with Ben?" Now Nick twisted the cloth into a semblance of a noose. His eyes went bright and hard as a dagger. "You introduced Fred to Stipley?"

"Sure." With a nod to a waitress, Zack began to fill another order. "He asked me who the pretty blonde was, so I introduced them. They hit it off, too."

"Hit it off," Nick repeated. "And you just let her walk out of here with a stranger."

"Come on, Nick, Ben's no stranger. We've known him for years."

"Yeah," Nick said grimly, imagining slipping the cloth noose around Zack's neck. "He hangs around bars."

Surprised and amused, Zack glanced over. "So do we."

"That's not the point, and you know it." Nick rattled bottles and resisted the urge to pour a stiff shot of whiskey for himself. "You can't just hook her up with some guy and let her waltz off with him."

"I didn't hook them up. I introduced them, they talked for a while and decided to catch a movie."

"Yeah, right." Movie, my ass, he thought. What man in his right mind would want to waste time at the movies with a woman with big, liquid gray eyes and a mouth like heaven? Oh, God, he thought, his stomach clenching as he imagined Fred at Ben Stipley's mercy. "Ben just wanted a little company at this week's box-office hit. Damn it, Zack, are you crazy?"

"Okay, I'll give it to you straight. I sold her to him for five hundred and season tickets to the Yankees. He should have her to the opium den by this time."

Nick managed to get his vivid imagination under control, but didn't have the same luck with his temper. "That's real funny, bro. Let's see how funny you are if he hits on her."

After setting the drinks aside, Zack turned to study his brother. Fury, he noted, which he'd seen plenty of times before on Nick's face. Since it seemed so incredibly out of place under the circumstances, he kept his tone mild.

"And if he does, she'll handle it or hit back. He's not a maniac."

"A lot you know about it," Nick muttered.

Baffled, Zack shook his head. "Nick, you like Ben. You've gone to Yankees games with him. He lent you his car when you wanted to drive to Long Island last month."

"Sure I like him." Incensed, Nick grabbed a beer mug from the shelf and began to polish it. "Why shouldn't I like him? But that has nothing to do with Fred picking up some strange guy in a bar and going off with him to God knows where."

Zack leaned back, tapping a finger against the bar.

"You know, little brother, someone who didn't know you might think you're jealous."

"Jealous?" Terrifying thought. "That's bull. Just bull." He slapped the mug down and chose another at random. If he didn't keep busy, he was afraid he might streak out of the bar and start searching every movie theater in Manhattan.

But a strange idea was beginning to take root in Zack's mind. He eyed Nick more cautiously now, toying with the thought of his brother falling for little Freddie Kimball.

"Then why don't you tell me what's not bull? What's going on with you and Freddie, Nick?"

"Nothing's going on." In defense, Nick concentrated on the glass he was polishing, and attacked. "I'm just trying to look out for her, that's all. Which is more than I can say for you."

"I guess I could have locked her up," Zack mused. "Or gone along with them as chaperon. Next time I see she's having a conversation with a friend of mine, I'll call the vice squad."

"Shut up, Zack."

"Cool off, Nick. Your Georgia peach just walked in."

"Great." Making an effort, Nick ordered himself to shift Freddie and her idiotic behavior to the back of his mind. He had his own life, didn't he? And, as Freddie had recently grown so fond of pointing out, she was a grown woman.

Nick glanced over, working up a smile, as Lorelie sauntered toward the bar. There she was, he thought.

Gorgeous, sexy, and if their last date was any indication, more than ready to let nature take its course.

She slid fluidly onto a bar stool, flipped back her shiny stream of dark hair and beamed sparkling blue eyes at him.

"Hello, Nick. I've been looking forward to tonight all day."

It was hard to keep the smile in place when it hit him—and it hit him hard—that he wasn't the least bit interested in southern hospitality.

Chapter Four

Nick smelled coffee and bacon the minute he stepped out of the shower. It should have put him in a better mood, but when a man hadn't slept well, worrying over a woman, it took more than the possibility of a hot meal to turn the tide.

She had a lot of explaining to do, he decided as he stalked into his bedroom to dress. Out half the night with some guy she'd picked up at a bar. She'd been raised better than that. He had firsthand knowledge.

It was one of the things he counted on, he thought as he met his own annoyed eyes in the mirror over the dresser. Freddie's family, the care and attention they devoted to each other. Every time he visited them, he'd seen it, felt it, admired it.

And he was just a little envious of it.

He'd missed that kind of care and attention growing up. His mother had been tired, and he supposed she'd been entitled to be, with the burden of raising a kid on her own. When she hooked up with Zack's old man, things had changed some. It had been good for a while, certainly better than it had been. They'd had a decent place to live, he mused. He'd never gone hungry again, or felt the terror of seeing despair in his mother's eyes.

With hindsight, he even believed that his mother and Muldoon had loved each other—maybe not passionately, maybe not romantically, but they'd cared enough to try to make a life together.

The old man had tried, Nick supposed as he tugged on jeans. But he'd been set in his ways, a tough old goat who never chose to see more than one side of things—his own side.

Still, there'd been Zack. He'd been patient, Nick remembered, carelessly kind, letting a kid trail along after him. Maybe it was the memory of that, the way Zack had taught him to play ball or just let him dog his heels, that had given Nick an affection and ease with children.

For he knew all too well what it was like, to be a kid and at the mercy of adult whims. Zack had made him feel as if he belonged, as if there were someone who would be there when you needed them to be there.

But it hadn't lasted. As soon as Zack was old enough to cut out, he had, joining the navy and shipping off. And leaving, Nick acknowledged now, a young stepbrother miserably alone.

When Nick's mother died, things had deteriorated fast. Nick's defense against the loss and the loneliness had been defiance, rebellion, and a replacement of family with the edgy loyalty of a gang.

So he'd been a Cobra, he reflected, cruising the streets and looking for trouble. Finding it. Until the old man died, and Zack came back to try to pull a bitter, hard-shelled kid out of the pit.

Nick hadn't made it easy on him. The memories of those days had a rueful smile tugging at his lips. If he could have found a way to make it harder back then, he would have. But Zack had stuck. Rachel had stuck. The whole chaotic bunch of Stanislaskis had stuck. They had changed his life. Maybe saved it.

It wasn't something Nick ever intended to forget.

Maybe it was his turn to do some paying back, he considered. Freddie might have the solid base he'd missed in his formative years, but she was flying free now. It seemed to him she needed someone to rein her in.

And since no one else was interested in overseeing Freddie's behavior, it fell to him.

He pulled his still-damp hair back and tugged a shirt over his head. Maybe she was just too naive to know better. He paused, considering the thought. After all, she'd spent most of her life snuggled up with her family in a little town where having clothes stolen off the line still made the papers. But if she was determined to live in New York, she had to learn the ropes fast. And he was just the man to teach her.

Feeling righteous, Nick strolled into the kitchen to begin the first lesson.

Freddie was standing at the stove, sautéing onions, mushrooms and peppers in preparation for the omelet she'd decided to cook as an opening apology. After a bit of reflection, she'd decided she'd been entirely too hard on Nick the day before.

It had been jealousy, she was forced to admit. Plain and simple.

Jealousy was a small, greedy emotion, she acknowledged to herself, and had no place in her relationship with Nick. He was free to see other women...for the time being.

Temper tantrums weren't going to advance her cause and win his heart, she reminded herself. She had to be open, understanding, supportive. Even if it killed her.

Catching the movement out of the corner of her eye, she turned to the doorway with a big, bright smile.

"Good morning. I thought you might want to start the day with a traditional breakfast for a change. Coffee's ready. Why don't you sit down, and I'll pour you some?"

He eyed her the way a man might a favored pet who tended to bite. "What's the deal, Fred?"

"Just breakfast." Still smiling, she poured coffee, then set the platter of toast and bacon on the table she'd already set. "I figured I owed you, after the way I acted yesterday."

She'd given him his opening. "Yeah, about that. I wanted to—"

"I was completely out of line," she continued, pouring already-beaten eggs into the sizzling pan. "I don't know what got into me. Nerves, I guess. I suppose I didn't realize how big a change I was making in my life, coming here."

"Well, yeah." Somewhat soothed, Nick sat and picked up a strip of bacon. "I can see that. But you've got to be careful, Fred. The consequences don't take nerves into account."

"Consequences?" Puzzled, she gave the fluffy eggs an expert flip. "Oh...I guess you could have booted me out, but that's a little excessive for one spat."

"Spat?" Now it was his turn to be puzzled, as she slid the omelet out of the pan. "You had a fight with Ben?"

"Ben?" She transferred the omelet to Nick's plate then stood holding the spatula. "Oh, Ben. No, why would I? Why would you think so?"

"You just said— What the hell are you talking about?"

"About yesterday. Giving you a hard time after Lorelie called." She tilted her head. "What are you talking about?"

"I'm talking about you letting some strange guy pick you up in a bar. That's what I'm talking about." Nick studied her as he forked in the first bite of his omelet. God, the kid could cook. "Are you crazy, or just stupid?"

"Excuse me?" All her good intentions began a slow slide into oblivion. "Are you talking about my going to the movies with a friend of Zack's?"

"Movies, hell." Nick fueled up on breakfast as he prepared to lecture. "You didn't get home until after one."

Her hands were on her hips now, and her fingers were tight around the handle of the spatula. "How would you know when I got home?"

"I happened to be in the neighborhood," he said loftily. "Saw you get out of a cab at the hotel. One-fifteen." The memory of standing on the street corner, watching her flit into the hotel in the middle of the night, soured his mood again, though it didn't diminish his appetite. "Are you going to try to tell me you caught a double feature?"

He reached for the jam for his toast just as Freddie brought the spatula down smartly on the top of his head. "Hey!"

"Spying on me. You've got a lot of nerve, Nicholas LeBeck."

"I wasn't spying on you. I was looking out for you, since you don't have the sense to look out for yourself." With well-conditioned reflexes, he ducked the second swipe, pushed back from the table. His body moved on automatic, tensed for a fight. "Put that damn thing down."

"I will not. And to think I felt guilty because I'd yelled at you."

"You should have felt guilty. And you sure as hell should have known better than to go off with some guy you know nothing about."

"Uncle Zack introduced us," she began, fury making her voice low and icy. "I'm not going to justify my social life to you."

That's what *she* thinks, Nick countered silently. No way in hell was he going to allow her to go dancing off with any bar bum who happened along, and he needed to make that clear. "You're going to have to justify it to somebody, and I'm the only one here. Where the hell did you go?"

"You want to know where I went? Fine. We left the bar and raced over to his place, where we spent the next several hours engaged in wild, violent sex—several acts of which are still, I believe, illegal in some states."

His eyes went hard enough to glitter. It wasn't just her words, it wasn't just her attitude. It was worse, because he could imagine—with no trouble at all—a scenario just like the one she'd described. Only it wasn't Ben she was breaking the law with. It was Nick LeBeck.

"That's not funny, Fred."

Much too wound up to note or care about the dangerous edge to his voice, she snarled at him. "It's none of your business where I went or how I spent my evening, any more than it's mine how you spent yours with Scarlett O'Hara."

"Lorelie," he corrected, between his teeth. It didn't do his disposition any good to remember that he hadn't spent the evening with Lorelie, or anyone else. "And it is my business. I'm responsible for—"

"Nothing," Freddie snapped back, jabbing the spatula into his chest. "For nothing, get it? I'm above the age of consent, and if I want to pick up six guys at a bar, you have nothing to say about it.

You're not my father, and it's about time you stopped trying to act like it.''

"I'm not your father," Nick agreed. A slow, vicious buzz was sounding in his ears, warning him that his temper was about to careen out of control. "Your father might not be able to tell you what happens to careless women. He sure as hell wouldn't be able to show you what happens when a woman like you takes chances with the wrong man."

"And you can."

"Damn right I can." In a move too quick and unexpected for her to evade, he snatched the spatula out of her hand and threw it aside. Even as it crashed against the wall, her eyes were going wide.

"Stop it."

"What are you going to do to make me?" Nick's movements were smooth, predatory, as he stalked her, backing her into a corner. "You going to call for help? You think anybody's going to pay attention to you?"

He'd never looked at her like that before. No one had, with all that lust and fury simmering. Fear lapped through her until her pulse was scrambling like a rabbit's.

"Don't be ridiculous," she said, trying for dignity and failing miserably as he slapped his palms on either side of the wall, caging her. "I said stop it, Nick."

"What if he doesn't listen to you?" He stepped closer, until his body was pressed hard against hers, until she could feel the wiry strength in it, just on the edge of control. "Maybe he wants a sample—

more than a sample. All that pretty skin.'' His eyes stayed on hers as he ran his hands up her arms, down again. ''He's going to take what he wants.'' Now his hands were at her hips, kneading. ''How are you going to stop him? What are you going to do about it?''

She didn't think, didn't question. Riding on fear jumbled with excitement, Freddie threw her arms around his neck. For an instant, the gleam in his eyes changed, darkened, and then her mouth was on his.

All her pent-up needs and fantasies poured into the kiss. She clung to him, wrapped herself around him and reveled in the wild flash of heat.

He was holding her as she'd always wanted to be held by him. Hard, possessively hard. His mouth was frantic as it took from hers. A scrape of teeth that made her head spin, a plunge of tongue that staggered her soul.

Desire. She could taste it on him. The full, ripe and ready-to-explode desire of a man for a woman. They might have been strangers, so new was this burst of passion and need. They might have been lovers for a lifetime, so seamlessly choreographed were the fast, frenetic movements of hands, of mouths and bodies.

He lost his head. Lost himself. Her mouth was a banquet of flavors—the tart, the sweet, the spicy— and he was ravenous. There was so much there— the scent and taste and texture of her, so much more than the expected, so much richer than dreams. All of it opened for him, invited him to feast.

He didn't think of who they were, or who they

had been. There was no thought at all, only a desperate leap of emotion that consumed him, even as he avidly consumed her.

More. The need for more slashed through him like a whip. He pressed her hips into the edge of the counter, then lifted her up onto it so that his hands were free to touch and take.

He heard her raspy indrawn breath when his fingers streaked under her sweater and closed over her. Then his own moan—part pain, part pleasure—when he found her, firm and soft, her nipples hard with desire against his thumbs, her heart pounding out an erotic rhythm against his palms.

She began to tremble. One quick shudder that grew and quickened until she was vibrating like a plucked string.

Shame washed over him, a cold gray mist over red-hot lust. Staggered by what he'd done, by what he'd wanted to do, he dropped his hands and slowly stepped back.

Her breath sounded more like sobbing, and her eyes, he noted, furious with himself, were glazed. As he watched, she gripped the edge of the counter for balance, and her knuckles went white.

"I'm sorry, Fred. Are you all right?" When she said nothing, nothing at all, he used his temper to combat the shame. "If you're not, you've nobody to blame but yourself. That's the kind of treatment you're opening yourself up to," he shot at her. "If it had been anybody but me, things would have been worse. I'm sorry I scared you, but I wanted to teach you a lesson."

"You did?" Though her heart was still thudding, Freddie was recovering, slowly. Nothing she ever imagined had come close to being as wonderful, as exhilarating, as the reality of Nick. Now he was going to spoil it with apologies and lectures. "I wonder—" hoping she could trust her legs, she slid slowly from the counter to the floor "—who taught whom. I kissed you, Nicholas. I kissed you and knocked you on your butt. You wanted me."

His blood was still humming. He couldn't quite silence the tune. "Let's not confuse things, Fred."

"Oh, I agree, let's not. You weren't kissing your little cousin just now, Nick. You were kissing me." Now it was she who stepped forward, and he back, in a reversal of the dance. "And I was kissing you."

His throat had gone unbearably dry. Who was this woman? he wondered. Who was this devilish sprite with eyes full of awareness and knowledge, who was turning him inside out with a look? "Maybe things got out of hand for a minute."

"No, they didn't."

The smile was entirely too smug and female. It was a look he recognized, and on another woman he might even have appreciated. "It isn't right, Fred."

"Why?"

"Because." He found himself fumbling over reasons he knew only too well. "I don't have to spell it out for you." He picked up his neglected coffee and drank it down stone-cold.

"I think you're having a hard time spelling it out for yourself." Empowered, Freddie tilted her head again. "I wonder, Nick, what *you* would do if I were to kiss you, right now."

Take her, he was certain, without thought or conscience, on the floor. "Cut it out, Fred. We both need to cool off."

"You may be right." Her lips curved again, sweetly. "I'd say you need some time to get used to the idea that you're attracted to me."

"I never said that." He set down his cup again.

"It isn't always easy to accept changes in people we think we know. But I've got plenty of time."

She was standing perfectly still, but he could feel her circling him. "Fred." He let out a long breath. "I'm trying to be reasonable here, and I'm not sure it's going to work." He frowned down at her. "I'm not sure any of this is going to work. Maybe some things have changed, and whatever those changes are, we don't seem to get along as smoothly as we once did. If working together means risking our friendship—"

"You're nervous about working with me?"

No button she could have chosen could have been more effective. Whatever he had made of himself through the years, there was still a remnant of the rebellious young man whose pride was a point of honor.

"Of course I'm not afraid of working with you, or anyone."

"If that's true, then we don't have a problem. Of course, if you're thinking you might not be able to stop yourself from— How did you so poetically put it? Oh, yes, sampling me—"

"I'm not going to touch you again."

The gritty fury in his voice only made her smile sweeten. "Well, then. I suggest you make the best of the breakfast you've let get cold. Then we'll get to work."

He was true to his word. They worked together for hours, and he never made any physical contact. It cost him. She had a way, he discovered, of shifting her body, tilting her head, looking up under her lashes—all of which seemed designed to make a sane man beg.

By the end of the day, Nick was no longer sure he was sane.

"That's good, good," Freddie murmured, scanning notes even as Nick played them. "Someone with Maddy O'Hurley's range is going to really kick on that."

"I didn't say this was Maddy's solo," Nick snapped. But that wasn't the point, he thought. The point was that Freddie was reading his mind, and his music, much too clearly. He had an odd and uncomfortable vision of himself as a fish nibbling at the bait. And it was Freddie holding the rod.

"Maybe I was thinking of using it for the second leads. A duet."

"No, you weren't," she said, calmly enough. "But fine, if you want to play it that way. I've got some ideas for lyrics for their number." She slid him a sidelong look. "They don't really fit this music, but I can adjust. Maybe if you pick up the tempo."

"I don't want to pick up the tempo. It's fine as it is."

"Not for the second leads' duet. Now, for Maddy's solo, it should go something like…'You made me forget, today and tomorrow, if you—'"

Nick interrupted her. "Are you trying to tick me off?"

"No, I'm trying to work with you." She made a quick note on one of the sheets of paper propped up on the piano, then shifted enough to smile at him. "I think you need a break."

"I know when I need a break." He snatched a pack of cigarettes off the top of the piano, lighted one. "Just shut up a minute, and let me work on this."

"Sure." With her tongue in her cheek, Freddie slid off the bench. She rolled her shoulders, stretched as he fiddled with the notes. Changing them, she noted, when they both knew they needed no changing.

He was fighting her, she noted, and realized nothing could have pleased her more. If he was fighting, that meant there was something there he had to defend against. Testing, she laid her hands on his shoulders and rubbed.

His system shot immediately into overdrive. "Cut it out, Fred."

"You're all stiff and tight."

His hands crashed down on the keys. "I said cut it out."

"Touchy," she murmured, but backed off. "I'm going to get something cold. Want anything?"

"Bring me a beer."

She lifted a brow, well aware that he rarely drank anything but coffee when he worked. As she stood in the kitchen opening a beer and a soft drink, she heard the quick rap on the door, the shout of greeting.

"You're busted," Alex Stanislaski called out from the other room. "For keeping my niece chained to a piano all afternoon."

"Where's your warrant, cop?"

Alex only grinned and caught Nick in a headlock. "I don't need no stinking warrant. Where is she, LeBeck?"

"Uncle Alex! Thank God you've come!" Freddie dashed into the living room and jumped into his arms. "It's been horrible. All day long, half notes, sharps, diminished ninths."

"There, there, baby, I'm here now." He gave her a quick kiss before holding her at arm's length. "Bess said you were prettier than ever. This guy been giving you a hard time?"

"Yes." She slipped an arm around her uncle's waist and smiled smugly at Nick. "I think you should haul him in for impersonating a human being."

"That bad, huh? Well, I'm here to take you away from all this. How about dinner?"

"I'd love it. Then you can tell me all about the promotion Bess was bragging about."

"It's nothing," Alex muttered, causing Nick to stop playing long enough to look over his shoulder.

"That's not what I heard." The sneer was automatic and friendly. *"Captain."*

"It's not official." Alex gave Nick a punch on the shoulder.

"Police brutality." Since Freddie hadn't brought it out, Nick rose to get his beer, and one for Alex from the kitchen. "He's always had it in for me."

"Should have tossed away the key the night I caught you climbing out of the window of that electronics shop."

"Cops have memories like elephants."

"When it comes to punks." Comfortable, Alex leaned against the piano. "That was a nice sound you were making. You two really collaborating on this musical thing?"

"That's the rumor," Freddie answered. "Only Nick's having a hard time splitting his energy between being my partner and my surrogate father."

"Oh?"

"He trailed me on a date last night."

"I did not." Disgusted, Nick took a swallow of beer. "She has delusions of adulthood."

A little wary of the vibes scooting around in the air, Alex cleared his throat. "She looks pretty grown up to me."

"Why, thank you. Same time tomorrow, Nick?"

"Yeah, fine."

"You can come on to dinner too, you know. The invitation was general," Alex said. "Bess is calling in Italian."

"No, thanks." Nick set aside his beer and ran his fingers over the keys. "I've got stuff to do."

"Suit yourself. Come on, Fred, I'm starved. I spent a hard day catching bad guys."

"I'm out the door." Deliberately she leaned over and kissed Nick's cheek. "See you tomorrow."

Alex waited until they'd gotten outside before he went for the subject. "So, what's going on?"

"On where?"

"Between you and Nick?"

"Not as much as I'd like," Freddie said without any preamble, and, since Alex merely stood there, stepped to the curb to hail a cab herself.

"Ah, are you speaking professionally, or personally?"

"Oh, professionally, we're clicking right along. He should have something to take the producers early next week. Why don't we take the subway?" she suggested after scanning the street. "It's going to be hell catching a cab this time of day."

He walked along with her toward the subway station. "You're talking...personally, then?"

"Hmm? That's right." She smiled approvingly over at him. The dimming sunlight haloed around his dark hair, making him look, to her, like a knight just out of battle. "It's so good to be here with all of you, Uncle Alex."

"It's good to have you. What kind of personally?" he asked, not allowing himself to be sidetracked for an instant from the subject at hand.

She sighed, but there was humor in it. "Exactly what you're worried about. I love you, Uncle Alex."

"I love you, too, Fred." He hurried after her as she started down the steps to the station. "Look, I know you had a crush on Nick when you were a kid.''

"Do you?" Only more amused, she dug around in her bag for change.

"Sure, it was kind of cute. We all noticed."

"Nick didn't." She let her change fall back into the bag when Alex pulled out tokens for both of them.

"So, he's slow. My point is, you're not a kid anymore."

She stopped on the other side of the turnstile, put both hands on his face and kissed him full on the mouth. "I can't tell you what it means to hear someone else say that. I *really* love you, Alexi."

"I think you're missing my point here." Taking her elbow, he guided her through the crowd waiting for the next train uptown.

"No, I'm not. You're worried that I'm going to do something that I'll regret, or that Nick will regret."

"If I thought he'd have anything to regret, he wouldn't be able to play a tune for a month."

She only laughed. "Big talk. You love him like a brother."

His golden eyes went dark. "It wouldn't stop me from breaking all the bones in his hands if he used them the wrong way."

She thought it best not to mention just where Nick's hands had been a few hours before. "I'm in love with him, Uncle Alex." She laughed, shaking back her hair. "Oh, that felt wonderful. You're the first one I've told. Dad and Mama don't even know." Her laugh leveled off to a chuckle when she saw that he was simply gaping at her. "Is it really that much of a surprise?"

He found his voice with an oath, then pulled her onto the train that had stopped at the station. "Now listen to me, Freddie—"

"No, listen to me first." Since the car was full, she snagged a pole and held on as the train jostled out of the station. "I know you're thinking I might not know the difference between puppy love and the real thing, but I do. I do," she repeated, with such quiet conviction that he remained silent. "I don't just love the boy I met all those years ago, Uncle Alex, or the one I came to know. It's the man he's become I'm speaking of. With all his faults, and his virtues, his impatience, his kindness, and even his streak of mean. I love the whole person, and he might not know it yet, he may not accept it, or love me back, but that doesn't change what's inside me for him."

Alex let out a long breath. "You have grown up."

"Yes, I have. And I've had the very best examples ahead of me. Not just Mama and Dad, but you and Bess and all the rest of you. So I know when you love deep enough, and true enough, it lasts."

He couldn't argue with that. What he'd found with Bess only became more precious and more vital every day. "Nick's as important to me as anyone in the family," Alex said carefully. "Even you. So I can tell you that he's not an easy man, Freddie. He's got baggage he hasn't tossed out."

"I know that. I can't say I understand it all, but

I know it. Just don't worry too much," she asked, and took one hand off the pole to touch his cheek. "And I'd appreciate it if you'd keep this between us for now. I'd like some time before the rest of the family starts looking over my shoulder."

When Freddie returned to the hotel that evening, there was a message waiting for her at the desk. Intrigued, she tore open the envelope as she took the elevator up to her floor.

Inside, Nick's handwriting was scrawled across a sheet of staff paper.

Okay, you're right. It's Maddy's solo. I want lyrics by tomorrow. Good ones. I've scheduled a meeting with Valentine and the rest of the suits. Don't mess up. Nick.

She all but danced to her room.

Two hours later, she was racing up the steps to Nick's apartment. She knew he was working the bar, and she couldn't be bothered with him. Instead, she sat at his piano and switched on the tape recorder.

"I've got your lyrics, Nicholas, and they're better than good. Just listen."

Primed by her own excitement, she sang to him as she played his melody. The words had been swimming in her head since she'd first heard the music. Refined now, polished, they melded with the notes as if they'd been born together.

After the last note died away, she closed her eyes.

"What are you doing here?"

She jolted, turning quickly toward the doorway, where Nick stood. He didn't look friendly, she noted.

"Leaving you a message. You wanted the song done before your meeting. It's done."

"I heard." And he'd suffered, listening to it, watching her as she sang for him. "Do you know what time it is?"

"About midnight, I guess. I thought you'd be busy downstairs."

"We are busy downstairs. Rio told me you were up here."

"You didn't have to come up. I just didn't want to wait until tomorrow." Her nerves came rushing back. "How much did you hear?"

"Enough."

"Well?" Impatient, she swung her legs over the bench so that she could face him. "What did you think?"

"I think they'll go for it."

"That's it. That's all you can say?"

"What do you want me to say?"

It was like pulling teeth, she thought, always. "What you feel."

He didn't know what he felt. She was somehow drawing him into areas he'd never explored. Never wanted to explore. "I think," he said carefully, "it's a stunning lyric, one that goes for the heart and the gut. And I think when people walk out of the theater, it'll be playing in their heads."

She couldn't speak. She was embarrassed when she realized that her eyes had filled. Lowering them, she stared at her linked hands. "That's a curve I didn't expect from you."

"You know the gift you have, Fred."

"Yes, I tell myself I do." Calmer, she looked up again. Her heart did one slow roll in her breast as she watched him. "I tell myself a lot of things, Nick. Things that don't always hold up when I'm alone in the middle of the night. But what you said will, whatever happens."

He couldn't take his eyes off her, hardly realized he was walking to her. "I'm going to take what we worked on so far to Valentine tomorrow. Take the day off."

"I can start on the new apartment while I'm trying not to go insane from nerves."

"Fine." As if it belonged to someone else, his hand reached down for hers, drew her to her feet. The only light in the room came from the gooseneck lamp atop the piano. Its glow fell short of them, leaving them in soft shadow. "You shouldn't have come back here tonight."

"Why?"

"I'm thinking about you too much. It's not the way I used to think about you."

"Times change," she said unsteadily. "So do people."

"You don't always want them to, and it's not always for the best. This isn't for the best," he murmured as he lowered his mouth to hers.

It wasn't frantic this time. She'd been prepared for that, but this time it was slow, and deep, and quietly desperate. Instead of revving for the storm, her body simply went limp, melting into his like candle wax left too long at the flame.

It was the innocence he felt, her innocence, fluttering helplessly against his own driving needs. The images that spun through his brain aroused him, amazed him, appalled him.

"I lied," he murmured, and pulled back with difficulty. "I said I wouldn't touch you again."

"I want you to touch me."

"I know." He kept his hands firm on her shoulders when she would have swayed toward him. "What I want is for you to go home, back to your hotel, now. I'll get in touch with you after I've seen Valentine."

"You want me to stay," she whispered. "You want to be with me."

"No, I don't." That, at least, was the truth. He didn't want it, even if he seemed so violently to need it. "We're family, Fred, and it looks as though we may be collaborators. I'm not going to ruin that. Neither are you." He set her aside, stepped away. "Now, I want you to go down and have Rio flag you a cab."

Every nerve ending in her body was on full alert. But while she might have preferred to scream in frustration, she could see that his eyes were troubled. "All right, Nick, I'll wait to hear from you."

She started for the door, then stopped and turned. "But you're still going to think about me, Nick. Too much. And it's never going to be the way it used to be again."

When the door closed behind her, he lowered himself to the piano stool. She was right, he acknowledged as he rubbed his hands over his face. Nothing was going to be quite the same again.

Chapter Five

Sunday dinner at the Stanislaski household was never a quiet, dignified affair. It began in the early afternoon, with the sounds of children shouting, adults arguing and dogs barking. Then there were always the scents of something wonderful streaming through the kitchen doorway.

As the family grew, the house in Brooklyn seemed to stretch at its joints to accommodate them all. Children tumbled over the floor or were welcomed into laps, and there were board games and toys scattered over the well-worn rugs. When it came time for the meal, leaves were added to the table and everyone sat elbow-to-elbow with everyone else in the chaos of conversation, bowls and platters being passed around.

Mikhail's and Sydney's home in Connecticut was

much larger, Rachel's and Zack's apartment more accommodating, and Alex's and Bess's airy loft more spacious. No one ever considered changing the tradition from Yuri's and Nadia's overflowing home.

Because this was where the family began, Freddie mused as she squeezed between Sydney and Zack on the ancient sofa. This, no matter where any of them lived or worked or moved to, was home.

"Up," Laurel demanded, and began the climb into Freddie's lap. She had the flashing sunburst smile of her father and her mother's cool, discerning eye.

"And up you go." Freddie bounced Laurel as the toddler entertained herself with the glint of colored stones on Freddie's necklace.

"You're pleased with the apartment, then?" Sydney reached out to run a hand over her son's hair as he darted past in pursuit of a cousin.

"More than pleased. I really appreciate you helping me out. It's exactly what I was looking for—size, location."

"Good." With a mother's instinct, Sydney kept a wary eye on her oldest. Just lately, he'd taken to torturing his sister. Not that she worried about Moira overmuch. The girl had a fast and wicked left jab. "Griff" she called out, and it took no more than that along with a steely maternal look, to have the boy reconsider yanking his sister's curling ponytail, just to see what would happen.

"Are you looking for furniture?" Sydney asked

as Laurel climbed determinedly from Freddie's lap to hers.

"Halfheartedly," Freddie admitted. There was a bloodcurdling war whoop from upstairs, followed by a loud thump. No one so much as blinked. "I picked up a few things over the last couple of days. I think I'll get more in the swing when I move in next week."

"Well, there's a shop downtown with good prices on rugs. I'll give you the name. Ah, Zack?"

"Hmm?" He tore his eyes from the ball game currently on the television and glanced in the direction Sydney indicated. His youngest had dragged a chair over to Nadia's breakfront and had both greedy eyes on a bag of Yuri's gumdrops, on the top shelf.

"Forget it, Gideon."

Gideon beamed, all innocence. "Just one, Daddy. Papa said."

"I'll just bet he did." Zack rose, caught his son around the waist and tossed him in the air to distract him. "Hey, Mom. Catch."

Experience and reflex had Rachel scooping her son out of the air on the fly. The new criminal court judge held her giggling child upside down as she turned to Freddie. "So, where's our temperamental Nick?"

Exactly the question Freddie had been asking herself. "I'm sure he'll be here shortly. He'd never miss a meal. I talked to him yesterday."

And he hadn't been able, or hadn't been willing, to give her an opinion on the producers' reaction to their collaboration. The wait, Freddie thought, was like sitting on one of Nadia's pin cushions.

Waiting was something she should excel at by now, she thought with a little sigh. She'd been waiting for Nick for ten years.

She let the conversation and noise flow around her before rising. Maneuvering with practiced skill around the various sprawled bodies and abandoned toys, she wandered into the kitchen.

Bess sat contentedly at the kitchen table, putting the finishing touches on an enormous salad while Nadia guarded the stove.

It was a good room, Freddie mused, looking around. A nurturing room, with its cluttered counters and its refrigerator door totally covered with wildly colorful drawings, courtesy of the grandchildren. Always there was something simmering on the stove, and the cookie jar was never empty.

Such things, she thought, such small things, made a home. One day, she promised herself, she would make such a room.

"Grandma." Freddie pressed a kiss to Nadia's warm cheek. She caught the scent of lavender weaving through the aromas of roasting meat. "Can I help?"

"No. You sit, have some wine. Too many cooks in my kitchen these days."

Bess winked at Freddie. "I'm only allowed because I'm getting lessons. Nadia thinks I should stop doing all my meals with the phone as my only cooking utensil."

"All my children cook," Nadia said with some pride.

"Nick doesn't," Freddie pointed out, and snatched a radish while Nadia's back was turned.

"I did not say they all cooked well." Nadia continued to mix the dough for her biscuits. She was a small, sturdy woman, her hair now iron gray, around a serene and timelessly lovely face. The smoothness, Freddie realized now, came from happiness. Age had scored a few lines, to be sure, but none came from discontent.

"When you learn," Nadia said, turning to wag a wooden spoon in Bess's direction, "you teach your children."

Bess gave a mock shudder. "Horrible thought. Just last week Carmen emptied an entire bag of flour over her head, then added eggs."

"You teach her right." Nadia smiled. "Your sons, too. I give you recipes my mama gave to me. Freddie, you make the chicken Kiev like I taught you?"

"Yes, Grandma." Unable to resist, Freddie gave Bess a smug smile. "When I'm settled in my new apartment, I'll cook it for you and Papa."

"Show-off," Bess muttered.

There were shouts from the other room, of greeting, of demands, of questions. As the noise level rose dramatically, Nadia opened her oven to check her roast.

"Nick is here," she announced. "Soon we eat."

In a move she hoped was casual, Freddie rose and

reached for the jug wine on the counter. "Want something cold, Aunt Bess?"

"I wouldn't mind some juice." With her tongue caught between her teeth, Bess sliced cucumbers with concentration and intensity. "How's the game going?"

"I was wondering about the same myself," Freddie murmured as the door of the kitchen swung open.

And there was Nick, a huge bouquet of daisies in one hand, a toddler in his other arm, and another child clinging to his leg.

"Sorry I'm late." He presented the bouquet to Nadia with a kiss.

"You bring me flowers so I don't scold you."

He grinned at her. "Did they work?"

She only laughed. "You're a bad boy, Nicholas. Put these in water. Use the good vase."

Unhampered by the children hanging on him, Nick opened a cabinet. "Pot roast," he said, and turned his head to nip at Laurel, on his hip. "Almost as tasty as little girls."

Laurel squealed happily and snuggled closer.

"Pick me up, Nick. Pick me up, too."

Nick looked down at the boy tugging on his jeans. "Wait until I have a hand free, Kyle."

"Kyle, let Nick finish what he's doing." Bess took the glass of juice Freddie offered.

"But, Mom, he picked Laurel up."

"Wait your turn." Nick dumped daisies into the vase, then bent to scoop the boy up. With his arms full again, he turned to look at Freddie. "Hi, kid. How's it going?"

"You tell me." She eyed him over the rim of her glass. And damned him for looking so casually beautiful, his hands full of children, his eyes impersonally friendly as they studied her. "Have you heard back from Reed?"

"It's Sunday," Nick reminded her. "He and his family are at the Hamptons, or Bar Harbor, or someplace. We'll hear something in a few days."

In a few days she would explode. "He must have had a reaction."

"Not really."

"Did he listen to the tape?"

Nick accommodated Kyle, who was squirming for attention, by tickling the boy's ribs. "Sure he listened."

In a lightning mood swing, Kyle shifted his affections and held out his arms and wailed for Freddie. The pass was completed with the fluidity of long practice, and she set him on her hip. "Well, then, what did he say when he heard it?"

"Not a lot."

She hissed through her teeth. "He must have said something. Indicated something."

Nick merely shrugged. He reached down, aiming for a slice of carrot from Bess's salad and got his hand slapped. "Jeez, Bess, who's going to notice?"

"I am. I'm working on presentation here. Color, texture, shape. Take this instead." She held out a carrot she had yet to slice.

"Thanks. Anyway, Fred, why don't you just play

house for a couple days?'' He bit into the carrot and chewed thoughtfully. He liked watching the way her eyes went from lake calm to stormy and the way her bottom lip seemed to grow fuller as temper took hold. ''Buy your knickknacks and whatever for the new place. I'll be in touch when I hear anything.''

''You just want me to wait?''

As if in sympathy, Kyle rested his head on Freddie's shoulder and scowled at Nick. ''You just want me to wait?'' he mimicked, and had Nick grinning.

''That's the idea. And don't get that devious brain of yours working on the idea of calling Valentine yourself. Old family friend or not, that's not how I work.''

She could only steam in silence, as that was exactly what she'd been considering. ''I don't see how it would hurt—''

''No,'' he said simply, and, handing her what was left of his carrot, walked out with Laurel.

''Stubborn, hardheaded know-it-all,'' Freddie grumbled.

''Know-it-all,'' Kyle echoed gleefully.

''Aunt Bess, when you have connections, you use them, don't you?''

Bess took a sudden, intense interest in the proper way to slice a mushroom. ''You know, I think I'm getting the hang of this. It's all in the wrist.''

''Temperamental jerk,'' Freddie said under her breath.

''Jerk,'' Kyle agreed, as she strode out with him on her hip.

"They are children one minute, men and women the next," Nadia commented.

"It's rough, being a grown-up."

Thoughtfully, Nadia rolled out her biscuit dough. "He looks at her."

Bess raised her head. She hadn't been certain Nadia would notice what she had. Of course, Bess mused, she should have known better. When it came to family, Nadia missed nothing.

"She looks back," Bess said, and the two women were suddenly grinning at each other.

"She would push him to be his best."

Bess nodded. "And he'd keep her from being too driven."

"He has such kindness in him. Such a need for family."

"They both do."

"It's good."

With a chuckle, Bess lifted her glass of juice. "It's great."

That was just the first of a number of conversations that night that both Freddie and Nick would have been stupefied to hear.

In their loft, Bess cuddled against Alex, sleepy-eyed and yawning. The first trimester of her pregnancies always left her as lazy as a cat in a moonbeam at night.

"Alexi."

"Hmmm?" He stroked her hair, half listening to the news on the bedroom television, half musing about his caseload. "Need something?"

It amused them both that she was the clichéd expectant mother in her early weeks, with all the accompanying strange cravings. "I think there are still some strawberries and peanut butter in the fridge."

"Well..." She thought it over, then shook her head. "No, we seem to be holding our own tonight." She smiled as his hand skimmed lightly over her still-flat belly. "Actually, I was thinking about Freddie and Nick."

Cautious, his promise to his niece weighing heavily on him, Alex shifted. "What about them?"

"Do you think they know they're crazy about each other, or are they still at that 'I don't know what's going on around here' stage?"

"What?" He sat straight up in bed, gaping down at his sleepy-eyed, tousled-haired wife. "What?"

"I can't decide myself." With ease, she slithered, accommodating herself to his new position. "It's probably a little weird for both of them, under the circumstances."

Alex let out a long breath. Why did he continue to delude himself that Bess's freewheeling manner made her oblivious of nuances?

"Weird," he muttered. "How do you know they're crazy about each other?"

She drummed up the energy to open one eye. "How many times do I have to tell you, writers are every bit as observant as cops? You noticed it, didn't you? The way they've started to look at each other, circle around?"

"Maybe." He wasn't certain he was entirely

comfortable with the idea yet. "Somebody ought to clue Natasha in."

Bess gave a lazy snort. "Alexi, compared to a mother, cops and writers are deaf, dumb and blind." She snuggled closer. "Strawberries, huh?"

Across town, Rachel and Zack made a final check on their kids. Rachel eased the headset off her daughter's ears while Zack tucked a stuffed rabbit more securely under her limp arm—a tribute, Rachel often thought, to the contrasts of a growing girl.

"She looks more like you every day," Zack murmured as they stood for a moment, watching their firstborn sleep.

"Except for that Muldoon chin," Rachel agreed. "Stubborn as stone."

Arm in arm, they walked out and across the hall, into the room shared by their sons. They both let out a long, helpless sigh. You could, if you were a parent and had particularly sharp eyes, just make out the two sprawled bodies amid the debris. Clothes, toys, models, sports equipment, were scattered, piled or precariously perched on nearly every surface on the top bunk, Jake's arm and leg draped over the mattress. A devoted guardian angel or pure good luck kept him from rolling over and falling into a heap on a tumble of possessions. Below, Gideon was no more than a lump beneath the tangled sheets.

"Are you sure they're ours?" Rachel wondered as she gave her older son a nudge that had him muttering in his sleep and rolling to safety.

"I ask myself that same question every day. I

caught Gideon telling one of Mik's kids that if they tied on bed sheets like a cape, then jumped off Yuri's roof, they'd fly back to Manhattan.''

Rachel closed her eyes and shuddered. "Don't tell me. Some things I'm better off not knowing." She uncovered Gideon's head on the pillow, discovered it was his feet, and tried the other side.

"I meant to ask you, how do you feel about Nick and Fred?"

"Working together? I think it's great." Zack swore as his stockinged foot stepped hard on an airplane propeller. "Damn it."

"I've told you to wear hip boots in here. And that's not what I meant. I meant how do you feel about the romance."

One hand massaging his wounded instep, Zack stopped dead. "What romance? Whose romance?"

"Nick and Fred. Keep up with the tour, Muldoon."

He straightened, very slowly. "What are you talking about?"

"About the fact that Freddie is head over heels in love with Nick. And the fact that he keeps shoving his hands into his pockets whenever she gets within arm's reach. Like he's afraid if he touches her he'll—"

"Hold on. Just hold on." Because his voice rose, she shushed him, and he grabbed her arm to pull her into the hall. "Are you telling me that the two of them are interested in—"

"I'd say they're way beyond interested."

Amused, Rachel tilted her head. "What's the matter, Muldoon? Worried about your baby brother?"

"No. Yes. No." Frustrated, he dragged a hand through his hair. "Are you sure about this?"

"Of course I am, and if you weren't so used to looking at Nick as if he were still a teenager with delinquent tendencies, you'd have seen it too."

Zack let his shoulders sag against the wall behind him. "Maybe I did see it. Something about the way he acted when she went out with this friend of ours."

Rachel's sense of fun kicked into high gear. "Uh-oh—jealous, was he? Sorry I missed it."

"He was ready to strangle me for introducing them." Slowly, Zack's lips curved. Then a laugh rumbled up. "Son of a gun. Freddie and Nick. Who'd have thought?"

"Anybody with eyes. She's been mooning over him for years."

"You're right. And she may be a sweetheart, but she's no pushover. I'd say my little brother has trouble on his hands." He looked back at his wife. Her hair was loose and tumbled. She was wearing only a thin robe that tended to slip, just a little bit, off her right shoulder. His grin widened. "And speaking of romance, Your Honor, I just had a thought, may it please the court."

Leaning forward, he whispered something in her ear that had her brows shooting up and her own mouth bowing. "Well, well, that's a very interesting suggestion, Muldoon. Why don't we discuss it—in my chambers?"

"Thought you'd never ask."

* * *

In their rambling house in the Connecticut countryside, Sydney lay sprawled over her husband. Her heart was still pounding like a jungle drum, her blood singing in harmony.

Amazing, she thought. After all these years, she never quite got used to just what the man could do to her body. She hoped she never would.

"Cold?" he murmured, skimming a hand over her naked back.

"Are you kidding?" She lifted her still-glowing face to his, meeting his eyes in the flickering glow of candlelight. "You're so beautiful, Mikhail."

"Don't start that."

She chuckled and trailed a line of kisses up his chest. "I love you, Mikhail."

"That you can start." He let out a contented sigh as she settled into the curve of his shoulder. For a time, they lay in blissful silence, watching the shadows dance.

"Do you think we will plan a wedding soon?" he asked.

Sydney didn't ask what wedding. Though they hadn't yet discussed it, she understood what he meant. And who. "Nick's not sure of his moves, or his needs. I think Freddie's sure of the latter for herself, but far from sure of the former. It's sweet, watching them watch each other."

"Reminds me of another time," he mused. "Another couple."

She shifted to smile at him. "Oh, does it?"

"You were very stubborn, *milaya.*"

"You were very arrogant."

"Yes." It didn't offend him in the least. "And if I had been less, you'd have been an old maid, married to your business." He barely registered the punch in the stomach. "But I saved you from that."

"Now who's going to save *you?*" She rolled on top of him.

Blissfully unaware of her family's interest, Freddie grabbed her just-hooked-up cordless phone in her new apartment. Almost dancing with excitement, she punched out the number quickly. Her father, she knew, would be in class, but her mother would be at the toy store.

"Mama." Clutching the receiver, she turned three circles, making her way across the living room toward the kitchen. "Guess where I am. Yes." Her laughter echoed through the nearly empty rooms. "It's wonderful. I can't wait for all of you to see it. Yes, I know, at the anniversary party. Everything's fabulous." She did a quick boogie over the antique Oriental she'd picked up in the shop Sydney had recommended. "I saw them all on Sunday. Grandma made pot roast. A present?" she stopped her improvised jitterbug to listen. "From Dad? Yes, I'll be here all day. What is it?"

She rolled her eyes and began a new dance. "All right, I'll be patient. Yes, I got the dishes you sent. Thank you. I even lined the kitchen cupboards to honor them. I've picked up some essentials."

She snagged a cookie from the bag on the kitchen

counter and two-stepped back into the living room. "No, I'm going to buy a bed here. I really hoped you'd keep mine in my room. It makes me feel like I'm still sort of there. Oh, and tell Brandon I haven't had a chance to get to Yankee Stadium yet, but I'm hoping to take in a game next week. And I've already got tickets for the ballet."

Two tickets, she thought. She'd get Nick there, come hell or high water.

"Tell Katie I'll commit every movement, every plié and fouettée turn to memory. Oh, and tell Dad— Oh, there's too much to tell everyone. I'll talk you all senseless when you come up, and— Hold on, someone's buzzing me. Yes, Mama," she said with a smile. "I'll make sure I know who it is first. Just wait. Yes?" she called into her intercom.

"Miss Frederica Kimball? Delivery for you."

"Papa?"

"Who you think?" came the strongly accented voice. "Frank Sinatra?"

"Come on up, Frankie. I'm in 5D."

"I know where you are, little girl."

"Yes, it's Papa," Freddie said into the phone. "He'll want to say hello, if you've got time." She was already unlocking her door and swinging it open. "You should see, Mama—I've got this great elevator, iron grates and everything. And my neighbor across the hall's a struggling poet who wears nothing but black and speaks in this tony British accent with just a hint of the Bronx underneath. I don't think she ever wears shoes. Oh, here's the elevator. Papa!"

It wasn't only Yuri. Behind him, Mikhail came, bearing an enormous box.

"Pots and pans," Mikhail told her when he set the box down with a dangerous-sounding thud. "Your grandma is afraid you don't have anything to cook with."

"Thanks. Mama's on the phone."

"Let me have it." Mikhail snatched the receiver even as her grandfather gathered Freddie into a bear hug.

Yuri was a big, broadly built man who squeezed her as if it had been years, rather than days, since he'd seen her.

"How is my baby?"

"Wonderful." He smelled of peppermint, tobacco and sweat, a combination she associated with love and perfect safety. "Let me give you the grand tour."

Yuri adjusted his belt, took one long, pursed-lipped look at her living room. "You need shelves."

"Well." She snuck her arm around his waist and fluttered her lashes. "Actually, I was thinking that if I just knew a carpenter who had some time..."

"I build you shelves. Where is furniture?"

"I'm picking it up, a little at a time."

"I have table in my shop. Goes well right here."

He stalked over to the windows, checked to see that they had adequate locks and moved smoothly up and down.

"Good," he pronounced. He was checking the baseboards and the level of the counters in the kitchcn when Nick strolled in. "So," Yuri said, "you come to unload boxes?"

"No." Nick shoved a large, blooming white African violet at Freddie. "Housewarming present."

She couldn't have been more thrilled if he'd come in on one knee, with a diamond ring the size of a spotlight in his hands. "It's beautiful."

"I remembered you liked plants. Figured you'd want one." With his hands already seeking the safety of his pockets, he scanned the room. "I thought you said it was just a little place."

It would fit two of his apartment, he noted, and shook his head. So went the perceptions of the rich and privileged. "You shouldn't leave your door open."

She lifted her brows. "I'm not exactly alone."

"Papa. Tash wants to talk to you. Fred, you got something to drink in here?"

"In the fridge," she told Mikhail, watching Nick. "So, did you come by to look the place over, give it the LeBeck seal of approval?"

"More or less." He wandered out of the living room, into the bedroom that held nothing more than a closet, which was already full of clothcs, a few boxes and a rug that he figured probably cost the equivalent of a year's rent for him.

"Where are you going to sleep?"

"I'm expecting a sofa bed to be delivered today. I want to take my time picking out a real bed."

"Hmmm." He wandered out again. Dangerous area, he realized. Thinking of her in bed. Her bed. His bed. Any bed. "You want to keep these windows locked," he said as he strolled through. "That fire escape's an invitation."

"I'm not an idiot, Nicholas."

"No, you're just green." He glanced up in time to catch the can of soda Mikhail tossed at him. "You need a dead bolt on that door."

"I have a locksmith coming at two. Anything else, Daddy?"

He only scowled at her. He was mulling over the proper retort when her buzzer sounded again. It seemed there was another delivery for Miss Kimball.

"Probably the sofa," Freddie mused, as Nick lighted a cigarette and looked around for an ashtray. She found him a porcelain soapdish shaped like a swan.

But it wasn't a sofa. Her mouth fell open and stayed open as three broad-shouldered men muscled in the base of a grand piano.

"Where you want it, lady?"

"Oh, God. Oh, my God. Dad." Her eyes filled to overflowing instantly.

"Put it over there," Nick told them as Freddie sniffled and wiped her cheeks. "A Steinway," he noted, thrilled for her. "Figures. Nothing but the best for our little Fred."

"Shut up, Nick." Still sniffling, she took the phone from Yuri. "Mama. Oh, Mama."

The men went about their business as she wept into the phone.

He should have left with the rest of them, Nick told himself when he found himself alone with Freddie thirty minutes later. She was busy tuning the glorious, gleaming instrument, between bouts of weeping.

"Cut it out, will you?" Shifting uncomfortably on the new bench, Nick hit middle C.

"Some of us have emotions and aren't ashamed to express them. Give me an A."

"God, what a piece," he murmured. "Makes my little spinet sound like a tin can."

She glanced over as she hit a chord. They both knew he could have replaced the spinet with an instrument every bit as magnificent as this. But he was attached to it.

"Looks like we'll be able to work here, too, if we want to." She waited a beat, flexed her fingers, tried out an arpeggio. "If we have anything to work on."

"Yeah, about that." Entranced with the piano, Nick began improvising a blues. "Listen to that tone."

"I am." As delighted as he, she picked up his rhythm and filled in on the bass. "About that?" she prompted.

"Hmm. Oh. You've got yourself a gig, Fred. You'll have contracts by the end of the week. You've lost the tempo," he complained when her hands faltered. "Pick it up."

She only sat, her hands still on the keys, staring straight ahead. "I can't breathe."

"Try sucking air in, blowing it out."

"I can't." Giving in, she swiveled, let her head fall between her knees. "They liked it," she managed as Nick awkwardly patted her back.

"They loved it. All of it. Valentine told me Maddy O'Hurley said it was the best opening number of her career, and she wanted more. She dug the love song, too. Of course, it was my melody that caught her."

"Cram it, LeBeck." But despite her sharp tone, her eyes were wet when she lifted her head.

"Don't start leaking again. You're a professional."

"I'm a songwriter." Jittery with success, she threw her arms around him and clung. "We're a team."

"Looks that way." He found his face buried in her hair. "You've got to stop wearing this stuff."

"What stuff?"

"That perfume. It's distracting."

She was too overwhelmed by possibilities to worry about taking careful steps. "I like distracting you." Heedlessly, she slid her lips up his throat until she found the vulnerable lobe of his ear and nipped.

He nearly gave in to the compelling need to turn his suddenly hungry mouth to hers, and swore. "Cut that out." Taking her firmly by the shoulders, he pushed her back. "We've got a professional relationship here. I don't want things clouded up with…"

"With what?"

"Hormones," he decided. "I'm past the age where I think with my glands, Fred, and you should be, too."

She ran her tongue over her lips. "Am I bothering your glands, Nicholas?"

"Shut up." He rose, knowing he was safer with some distance. "What we need is some ground rules."

"Fine." She couldn't stop the wide smile or the sparkle in her eyes. "What are they?"

"I'll let you know. Meanwhile, we're partners. Business partners." He decided it wasn't wise to seal the arrangement with a handshake. Not when she had those soft, narrow, incredibly sensitive hands. "Professionals."

"Professionals," she agreed. She tilted her head and crossed her legs in a slow, fluid way that had him staring carefully at a spot above her head. "So, when do we start...partner?"

Chapter Six

Nick knew Freddie's mind wasn't focused on her work. They'd cruised along smoothly enough for two weeks, but as the time approached for her family to come to New York for Nadia's and Yuri's anniversary party, her work came more in fits and starts than in a flow.

He hadn't meant to snap at her, really, but the way her mind was darting from subject to subject— a new recipe for canapés she just had to give to Rio, the art deco lamp she'd bought for her living room, the jumpy, tongue-twisting lyrics she'd come up with for a number in the second act—they weren't getting any real work done.

"Why don't you just go shopping, get your nails done, do something really important."

Freddie sent him a bland look and forced herself

not to look at her watch again. Her family was scheduled to arrive in less than three hours.

"I bet Stephen Sondheim's taking an afternoon off wouldn't have sent Broadway into a crisis."

He knew that. And if she hadn't *assumed* they were taking the rest of the day off, he'd have suggested it himself. "We've got an obligation. I take obligations seriously."

"So do I. I'm only talking about a few hours."

"A few hours here, a few hours there." He refused to look at her as he reached up to change a note on the sheet of music. "You've already had plenty of those the last few days." He picked up the cigarette he'd left burning and drew deep. "It must play hell, having your social life get in the way of your hobby."

She took a careful breath, hoping it would help. It didn't. "It must play hell, having your creativity always at war with your sanctimonious streak."

That little barb stung, as she'd meant it to. "Why don't you try doing your job? I can't keep carrying you."

Now her breath hissed out. "Nobody has to carry me. I'm here, aren't I?"

"For a change." He tossed the cigarette back in the ashtray to smolder. "Now why don't you try contributing something, so we can earn our keep? Some of us don't have Daddy's money behind us, and have to work for a living."

"That's not fair."

"That's the fact, kid. And I don't want a partner

who only wants to play at songwriting when it suits her busy schedule.''

Freddie pushed back on the stool, swiveled—the better to glare at him. ''I've been working every bit as hard as you, seven days a week for nearly three weeks now.''

''Except when you had to go buy sheets, or a lamp, or wait for your bed to be delivered.''

He was baiting her, and even knowing it, she swallowed the lure whole. ''I wouldn't have had to take time off if you'd agreed to work at my place.''

''Yeah, great. Working with all the sawdust and noise, while Yuri builds you shelves.''

''I need shelves.'' She did her best to rein in the temper he seemed hell-bent on driving to a gallop. ''And it was hardly my fault that the delivery was three hours late. I finished the chorus from the first solo in the second act while I was there.''

''I told you that needs work.'' Ignoring her, Nick started to play again.

''It's fine.''

''It needs work.''

She let out a huff of breath, but she refused to lower herself to the childish level of arguing back and forth. ''All right, I'll work on it. It would help if the melody wasn't flat.''

That tore it. ''Don't tell me the melody's flat. If you can't figure out how to write for it, I'll do it myself.''

''Oh, really? And you've got such a way with words, too.'' Sarcasm dripped as she rose from the bench. "Go ahead, then, Lord Byron, write us some poetry."

When his eyes snapped to hers, they were dangerously sharp and ready to slice. "Don't throw your fancy education in my face, Fred. Going to college doesn't make you a songwriter, and neither do connections. I'm giving you a break here, and the least you can do is put in the time it takes."

"You're giving me a break." There was a growl in her voice, feral and furious. "You conceited, self-important idiot. All you've given me is grief. I make my own breaks. I don't need you for this. And if you're not satisfied with my work habits, or the results, take it to the producers."

She stormed across the room, snatching up her bag en route.

"Where the hell do you think you're going?"

"To get my nails done," she tossed back, and made it to the door before he caught her.

"We're not done here. Now sit down and do what you're getting paid to do."

She would have shaken him off, but after one attempt, she decided she preferred dignity to freedom. "Let's get something straight here. We're partners. Partners, Nicholas, which means you are *not* my boss. Don't confuse the fact that I've let you call the shots so far with subservience."

"You've *let* me call the shots," Nick repeated, enunciating each word.

"That's exactly right. And I've tolerated your mercurial moods, your sloppiness, and your indulgent habit of sleeping until after noon. Tolerated them because I chose to attribute them to creativity. I'll work in this sty you live in, arrange my schedule to accommodate yours, even struggle to make something worthwhile out of second-rate melodies. But I won't tolerate nasty remarks, insults or threats.''

His eyes were glittering now. Another time, she might have admired the golden lights among the green. ''Nobody's threatened you. Yet. Now, if you've got your little tantrum out of your system, let's get back to work.''

She jabbed her elbow into his ribs, remembering his advice about putting her body behind it. He was still swearing when she yanked the door open.

''You go to hell,'' she suggested, and slammed the door hard in his face.

He nearly, very nearly, went after her. But he wasn't entirely sure whether he would strangle her or drag her off to bed. Either way, it would be a mistake.

What had gotten into her? he wondered as he nursed his sore ribs on the way back to the piano. The girl he'd known had always been agreeable, a little shy, and as sweet-natured as a sunrise.

Showed what happened, he supposed, when little girls became women. A little constructive criticism, and they turned into shrews.

Damn it, the chorus did need work. The lyrics weren't up to her usual standard. And, as he would be the first to admit, her usual standard was stunning.

Thoughtfully, he ran a hand along the edge of the piano. Well, maybe he hadn't admitted it. Not exactly. But she knew how he felt. She was supposed to know how he felt.

Disgusted, he rubbed at a headache brewing dead center in his forehead. Maybe he'd been a little hard on her, but she needed somebody to crack the whip now and then. She'd been pampered and indulged all of her life, hadn't she? It showed in the way she would carelessly shift priorities from work to social issues.

How long did it take for anyone to set up house-keeping? After Rachel and Zack moved out, he'd been settled in fine in a couple of hours.

Frowning now, Nick turned on the bench to face the room. So it was a little messy—it was lived-in, homey.

No, the place was a sty. He'd meant to pick it up, but since it never stayed that way, what was the point? And he'd planned to paint, and maybe get rid of that chair with the broken leg at some point.

It was no big deal; he could take care of it in a weekend. He didn't need the kind of palace Freddie was setting up a few blocks away. He could work anywhere.

It was irritating that the more time she spent in these rooms, the more drab and unkempt they seemed to him. But it was his business, and he didn't need her making snide comments about the way he chose to live.

Determined to push her out of his mind, he set his fingers on the keys, began to play. After two bars, his face was grim.

Damn it, the melody was flat.

* * *

In her apartment, Freddie put the finishing touches on the welcome snack she was preparing for her family. Already she was regretting not holding out for a larger place. If she had rented a two-bedroom, everyone could have stayed with her instead of bunking in with Alex and Bess.

Still, they'd all have some time together at her place before the party, and she wanted it to be perfect.

Your problem exactly, she mused, and her shoulders slumped as she arranged fruit and cheese. Everything always has to be perfect to satisfy Fred. Good isn't enough. Wonderful isn't enough. Perfection only, or toss it out.

She'd swiped at Nick because he wasn't perfect.

He'd deserved it, though, she assured herself. Making her sound like some spoiled child who was only playing at a career. That had hurt, hurt more because she wanted his respect every bit as much as she wanted his love. The hurt continued to ache because he hadn't understood, didn't understand how very much it all meant to her.

Coming to New York was a thrill, true, but it had also been a wrench to her heart. Writing the score for the musical was a dream come true, but it was also grueling work, with the sharp terror of failure always balanced over her head like an ax.

Didn't he know that if she failed as his partner, she would have failed at everything she'd ever wanted? It wasn't just a job to her, and it certainly wasn't the hobby he'd made it sound like. It was, very simply, her life.

Because thinking of it made her eyes sting, she fought to put it out of her mind and concentrate on the evening ahead.

It would be perfect— Catching herself, she swore, and then nearly sliced her finger instead of the stalk of celery. It would be wonderful, she corrected, having the whole family in one place, celebrating the endurance and beauty of marriage. Because it was important to her, she'd taken on a great deal of the responsibility for planning Yuri's and Nadia's anniversary celebration herself. She'd chosen and ordered the flowers, helped Rio select the menu, and worked out countless other details.

While Nick was sleeping that morning, she'd already been at Lower the Boom, decorating the bar. She and Rachel and Zack had scrubbed the place down first, so that every inch would shine. Bess had helped her with the balloons, and Alex had taken an hour's personal time to pitch in. Sydney and Mikhail had swung by to help Rio with kitchen duty.

Everyone had helped, she thought now. Except for Nick.

No, she wasn't going to think about him, she promised herself. She was only going to think about how they would all make the evening as special for her grandparents as it could possibly be.

When her buzzer sounded, she raced to it, her eyes darting everywhere, to make sure all was in place.

"Yes?"

"The Kimball crew, all present and accounted for."

"Dad! You're early. Come up, come on up. Fifth floor."

"On our way."

Freddie hurried to the door, dragging at locks, pulling at the safety chain. Unable to wait, she raced out to the elevator, fidgeting as she heard its mechanical whine.

She saw them behind the grate first, when the car came to a stop—her father's gold hair, with its gleaming threads of silver, her mother's dark, dancing eyes. Brandon with a Yankees cap on backward and Katie already tugging at the grate.

"Fred, what a great place." Already as tall as her sister, Katie threw her long, graceful arms around Freddie's neck. "There's a dance studio across the street. I could see them rehearsing through the window."

"Big deal," Brandon said. "Where's the food?"

"Ready and waiting," she assured him. Brandon was, she thought, a spectacular melding of their parents, gold and exotic. "Door's open." She accepted his quick, offhand kiss as he brushed by her.

"Dad." She giggled, as she always had, when he scooped her off her feet for a hug. "Oh, it's so good to see you. I've missed you." She blinked back tears she hadn't expected as she reached out for Natasha. "I've missed you both so much."

"The house isn't the same without you." Natasha rocked in the tight embrace, then eased back. "But look at you! So sleek and polished. Spence, where's our little girl?"

"She's still in there." He bent to kiss Freddie again. "We brought you something."

"More presents?" She laughed and slipped her arms around their waists to lead them to the apartment. "I haven't gotten over the piano yet. Dad, it's beautiful."

He nodded as he stood in the doorway and studied it. The dark wood gleamed in the sunlight from the window. "You chose the right spot for it."

She started to tell him that Nick had chosen the spot, then shook her head instead. "There couldn't be a wrong one."

"You got anything but rabbit food?" Brandon demanded as he strolled out of the kitchen gnawing on a celery stick.

"That's all you're getting here. You can stuff yourself at the party."

"Mama, Dad," Katie called out from the bedroom. "Come here. You've got to get a load of this!"

"My bed," Freddie explained to her puzzled parents. "It just came yesterday."

It was, if she said so herself, utterly fabulous. The spacious room had allowed her to indulge in kingsize, and she'd chosen a head and footboard of iron, painted a soft green, like copper patinated over time. The rods curved in a graceful semicircle, and were accented by metal flowers and small exotic birds in flight.

"Wow" was all Brandon could say with his mouth full of the scorned rabbit food.

"Great, isn't it?" Lovingly Freddie ran her fingers over the bars, and along the ivory-toned lace of the spread she'd chosen.

"Like sleeping in a fairy tale," Natasha murmured.

"Exactly." Freddie beamed. If anyone would understand and appreciate the sentiment, she knew it would be her mother. "And Papa built the shelves here for the carvings Uncle Mik made me over the years. I picked up this mirror at an antique shop downtown." She glanced at the ornately framed glass, its long oval shape accented by twisting brass-and-copper calla lilies, then grimaced at the cardboard boxes beneath.

"I haven't found the right bureau yet."

"You've accomplished a lot in less than a month," Spence pointed out. There was a little ache, just under his heart. He expected it would always be there when he thought of his baby living away from him. But there was pride, as well, and that was what showed in his eyes as he draped an arm around her shoulders. "I hear you and Nick are making progress on the score."

"It comes and goes." Forcing a smile, she walked back to the living room, where Brandon was already sprawled on the sofa and Katie was darting from window to window, hoping for another glimpse of the dance rehearsal.

"I still need to change for the party," Freddie said a little later, after they made a thorough inspection and caught each other up on their current events. "We'll need to get there early. You have the tickets, Dad?"

"Right here." He patted the breast of his jacket. "Two to Paris, open-dated, with a certificate for a stay at the honeymoon suite at the Ritz."

"Mama and Papa in Paris," Natasha murmured. "After all these years, for them to go back to Europe like this."

Gently Spence brushed a hand over her dark cork-screw curls. "Not quite as exciting as traveling through the mountains in a wagon."

"No." She smiled. The memory of their escape from the Ukraine, the fear and the bitter, bitter cold, had never faded. "But I think they'll prefer it." She noted, as she had several times over the past hour, the trouble lurking in Freddie's eyes. "I think you and the kids should go over now, Spence, see if Zack and Nick need any help." She smiled again, sending a silent message to her husband. "I'll stay here and primp with Freddie."

Curiosity came and went in his eyes before he nodded. "Sounds like a plan. Save the first dance for me," he added, kissing his wife.

"Always." Natasha waited, nudging her younger children along, then accepting Freddie's offer of a glass of wine. "Show me what you'll wear tonight."

"When I bought it I figured wearing it tonight would make me the sexiest woman there." Pride glowed on her face as she studied her mother, exotic as a Gypsy in flowing carmine silk. "After seeing you, I guess I'll have to settle for the second sexiest."

With a quick, throaty laugh, Natasha led the way

into the bedroom. "Don't mention looking sexy around your father. He isn't quite ready for it."

"But he's all right, isn't he? About the move?"

"He misses you, and sometimes he looks in your room as if he still expects to see you there—in pigtails. So do I," Natasha admitted, and sat on the edge of the bed. "But yes, he's all right with it. More than. He—both of us are so proud of you. Not just because of the music, but because of who you are."

No one was more surprised than Natasha when Freddie dropped on the bed beside her and burst into tears.

"Oh, my love, my baby, what is it?" Drawing Freddie close, Natasha stroked and soothed. "There, sweetheart, tell Mama."

"I'm sorry." Giving up, Freddie pressed her face into Natasha's soft, welcoming shoulder and wept. "I guess this has been building up all day—all week. All my life. Maybe I am spoiled and indulged."

Instantly insulted, Natasha leaned back to look at Freddie. "Spoiled? You're not spoiled, and not indulged! What would put such nonsense in your head?"

"Not what, who." Disgusted with herself, Freddie dug around in her pocket for a tissue. "Oh, Mama, I had such an awful fight with Nick today."

Of course, Natasha thought with a little inward sigh. She should have suspected it. "We often fight with those we care about, Freddie. You shouldn't take it so hard."

"It wasn't just a spat, not like we've had before. We said awful things to each other. He doesn't have any respect for who I am, or what I'm trying to do. As far as he's concerned, I'm just here to kick up my heels, knowing if I trip, you and Dad will be there to catch me."

"And so we would, if you needed us. That's what family is for. It doesn't mean you're not strong and self-reliant, just because you have someone who would reach out if you needed help."

"I know. I know that." But it helped enormously to hear it, all the same. "He just thinks— Oh, I wish I didn't care what he thought," Freddie added bitterly. "But I love him. I love him so much."

"I know," Natasha said gently.

"No, Mama." Taking a steadying breath, Freddie shifted so that her eyes were level with Natasha's. "It's not like with Brandon and Katie, or the rest of the cousins. I love him."

"I know." The ache in Natasha's own heart swelled as she smoothed back Freddie's tumbled hair. "Did you think I wouldn't see it? You stopped loving him as a child loves years ago. And it hurts."

Comforted, Freddie rested her head on Natasha's shoulder again. "I didn't think it was supposed to. It was always so easy to love him before." She sniffled. "Now look at me, crying like a baby."

"You have emotions, don't you? You have a right to express them."

She had to smile, as her mother's words so closely echoed the ones she herself had thrown at Nick days before. "I certainly expressed them this afternoon. I told him he was sloppy and self-important."

"Well, he is."

With a watery chuckle, Freddie got up to pace. "Damn right he is. He's also kind and generous and loving. It's just hard to see it sometimes, through that shell he's still got covering him."

"His life hasn't been simple, Freddie."

"And mine has." She reached out to trace the carving of a sleeping princess Mikhail had made her with her finger. "Dad worked hard to give me the kind of home every child should have. And then you came and completed the circle. You and the whole family. I know Nick was already a man when we came into his life, and that the years before left scars. It's the whole person I'm in love with, Mama."

"Then you'll have to learn to accept and deal with the whole person."

"I'm beginning to understand that. I had it all worked out," she said, turning with a wry smile on her face. "I had a carefully outlined plan. But it's not a simple thing, convincing a man to fall in love with you."

"Do you really want it to be simple?"

"I thought I did. Now I don't know what I want or what to do about it."

"You can make one part simple." Rising, Natasha took the tattered tissue from Freddie's hand and dried her daughter's tears herself. "Be yourself. Be true to that, to your heart. Patience." She laughed when Freddie rolled her eyes. "I know that's difficult for you. But patience, Freddie. See what happens if you step back instead of bounding forward. If he comes to you, you'll have what you want.''

"Patience." More settled, Freddie heaved an exaggerated sigh. "I guess I could try it." She cocked her head. "Mama, am I bossy?"

"Perhaps a little."

"Stubborn?"

Natasha tucked her tongue in her cheek. "Perhaps more than a little."

Amused at herself, Freddie smiled. "Flaws or virtues?"

"Both." Natasha kissed Freddie's nose. "I wouldn't change either trait. A woman in love needs to be a little bossy, and more than a little stubborn. Now go wash your face. You're going to make yourself beautiful—and make him suffer."

"Good idea."

Nick decided he wouldn't hold a grudge. Since it was Yuri's and Nadia's night, he wouldn't spoil it by sniping at Fred. However much she deserved it.

And maybe, just maybe, he felt a little guilty. Especially after coming downstairs and seeing firsthand how much time and effort she'd put into making the place festive. If someone had bothered to wake him up, he'd have given her a hand. With a flick of his finger, he sent the lacy white wedding bells over the bar spinning.

He wouldn't have thought of wedding bells, he admitted. Or of the baskets and buckets of flowers that filled the room with color and scent. He wouldn't have come up with the feathery doves hanging from the ceiling or the elegant candles in silver holders at the tables.

It would have taken her a lot of time to track down the decorations, he supposed. So maybe he should have been a little more patient with her dashing out on him, or dashing in with her mind so obviously elsewhere.

He'd forgive her, and let bygones be bygones.

"Hey, Nick, did you try those meatballs?"

He turned, cocked a smile at Brandon. "I saw them, and nearly got my hand chopped off reaching for a sample."

"Rio likes me better." Smug, Brandon slid a meatball from a toothpick into his mouth. "Hey, did you get a load of Freddie's bed?"

"Her bed?" Guilt, fear and secret lust sharpened his voice. "Of course not. Why would I?"

"It's a real piece of work, big as a lake." Brandon slid onto a stool and tried his most charming smile. "So, Nick, how about a beer?"

"Don't mind if I do."

"I meant for me," Brandon complained when Nick helped himself.

"Sure, kid. In your dreams." He glanced over as the door opened. And was very grateful he'd already swallowed.

Natasha was striking, an elegant Gypsy in swirling red silk, but Nick's gaze was riveted to Freddie.

She looked as though she'd draped herself in moonlight. He tried to tell himself the dress was gray, but it glinted and danced with silver lights. And she was poured into it. The simple scooped neckline and snugly cinched waist enhanced her slim, fragile build. And the way her hair was left loose and tousled made it appear she'd just gotten out of that lake-size bed Brandon had just told him about.

Natasha immediately walked over to hug him, and Freddie offered him a quick, distant smile but avoided meeting his eyes.

"New suit?" Freddie asked at random, realizing she had to say something and she'd been staring at his lapel for several seconds. She approved of the tailored lines of the black jacket, but certainly wasn't going to say anything about it.

"I figured the occasion called for it."

But not for a tie, she noted. The open collar of the black shirt suited him—as did the beer in his hand and the challenging glint in his eyes when she finally looked up. She hoped her careless shrug masked her thoughts of just how dangerous—and exciting—he looked. The man didn't deserve her compliments, after his behavior that day.

"You look very handsome," Natasha put in.

"Thanks."

"Everything looks perfect. I had a wonderful time arranging it all," Freddie said, turning a slow circle to be certain everything was in place.

"You did a good job in here." It was, Nick thought, a suitable white flag. But she only tossed him a carefully bland look over her shoulder. "It looks great," he continued, wishing he'd kept his mouth shut in the first place. "Must have taken a lot of time."

"I've got nothing but time, according to some people. Brandon, how about giving me a hand? Uncle Mik will be bringing Papa and Grandma along any time."

"He's not bringing them," Nick muttered into his beer.

"What do you mean, he's not bringing them? Of course he is. I arranged it."

"I unarranged it," Nick shot back, then added, "they're coming in a limo."

She blinked. "A limo?"

"I got the idea from someone," he said, and sent her a sneer. "It's their anniversary, after all. It's not like they're just going out to dinner."

Freddie made a sound in her throat that had Brandon wiggling his eyebrows at his mother.

"Battle stations," he murmured, and leaned forward to enjoy the fray.

"That was very considerate of you, Nicholas." Freddie's voice was cool and controlled again, causing her brother to sigh in disappointment. "I'm sure they'll appreciate it. And, of course, it takes hardly any time and effort at all to pick up the phone and order a car. I'm going to help Rio."

She sashayed out. Or so Nick described it to himself. Muttering, he pushed aside his beer. It looked as though it were going to be a very long night.

Chapter Seven

Freddie hated the fact that she couldn't stay mad at Nick. Aloof, maybe. The bar was crowded with so many bodies, the room filled with so much noise, that it wasn't difficult to stay aloof from one man.

But she just couldn't hold on to her temper, not after what Nick had done for her grandparents.

In any case, there wasn't time to brood over it, or over him. There were toasts to be drunk, food to be eaten, dances to be danced.

Not that Nick asked her to dance. He partnered her aunts, her mother, Nadia, family friends and relations. And, of course, the stupendously sexy Lorelie.

Well, if he was playing the aloof game, she would play harder.

"Great party!" Ben shouted near her ear.

"It is." She managed to work up a smile for him as he awkwardly led her around the crowded dance floor. "I'm glad you could make it."

"Wouldn't have missed it. I've known Zack's in-laws for years. Terrific people."

"The best." Her smile bloomed a bit when she spotted Alex twirling his mother. "The very best."

"I was thinking…" Ben missed a step, and barely missed her toes. "Sorry. Failed my dance class."

"You're doing fine." Though he was in danger of breaking her wrist as he pumped her arm like a well handle to keep his time. She grabbed the first distraction she could think of to save herself. "Have you tried the food? Rio's really outdone himself."

"Then let's get some plates."

Look at her, Nick thought darkly, scowling at Freddie as Lorelie draped herself over him. Flirting with Ben. Anyone—even Ben—should have the sense to see that she wasn't interested. Just leading him on. Typical female.

"Nick, honey." Lorelie's creamy voice invaded his thoughts. She sent him a melting look. "You're not paying attention. I feel like I'm dancing by myself."

He sent her a quick, charming smile that made even the savvy Lorelie almost believe he thought of no one but her. "I was just wondering if I should check the bar."

"You checked it five minutes ago." Lorelie pouted prettily. She knew when she didn't have a man's full attention—and how to take it philosophically. As attractive as Nick was, there were always other fish to fry. "Well, why don't you get me a glass of champagne, then?"

"Sure, coming right up." Relieved, he left her. She'd been clinging to him all night, like poison ivy on an oak, Nick thought. That kind of possessiveness always made him determined to shake loose.

The truth was, they just weren't clicking. He didn't think he was going to break her heart or anything quite so melodramatic, but Nick had learned through sad experience that women didn't always take even the most compassionate breakup well.

He'd have to let her down gently. No doubt, the sooner he backed off, the better it would be. For her.

The idea made him feel so altruistic, and relieved, that he opened a fresh bottle of champagne with a celebratory pop.

"How come we get music only from that box?" Yuri caught Nick in a headlock that would have felled a grizzly. "Are you a piano player or not?"

"Sure, but I'm kind of tied up here."

"I want music from my family. It's my party, yes?"

The man who could deny a request from Yuri was a tougher man than Nick LeBeck.

"You bet, Papa. I'll get right on it. Here take this." He handed Yuri the glass of champagne. "No, don't drink it." With a quick laugh, Nick gestured across the room. "See the brunette over there? The one with the big…personality?"

Yuri grinned lavishly. "Who could miss?"

"Take it to her, will you? Explain I'll be playing for a while. And don't lay on too much charm."

"I'm very controlled." Then he rhumbaed over to Lorelie.

Prepared to enjoy himself, Nick made his way through the crowd to the piano. His smile dimmed considerably when he spotted Freddie already sitting on the bench.

"You're in my spot."

She shot him a look that said in no uncertain terms that she was no more pleased with the arrangement than he. "They want both of us."

"It only takes one."

"It's Papa's party, yes?"

He caught himself struggling with a grin at her imitation. "Looks that way. Move over."

He sat, deliberately shifting to avoid touching her tempting, creamy shoulder and angled toward the keyboard beside the piano.

"What do they want?"

"Cole Porter, maybe, or Gershwin."

With a grunt, Nick began the opening bars of "Embraceable You."

Freddie shrugged and flowed with him into the tune.

Twenty minutes later, she was too pleased with the partnership to attempt to be aloof. "Not too shabby."

"I can hold my own with forties stuff."

"Hmm." Automatically she picked up on the boogie-woogie he'd slid into.

He was enjoying, too much, the way she always seemed to anticipate him in any improvisation.

And her perfume was driving him insane.

"You can take five if you want. I can handle this. Ben's probably getting lonely."

"Ben?" Blank, she glanced up again. "Oh, Ben. I think he can survive without me. But you go ahead and take a break. I'm sure Lorelie misses you."

"She's not the possessive type." To cover the lie, he switched tempos, trying to catch her. But she kept pace with him easily.

"Really? Couldn't prove that by me, the way she was hanging all over you. Of course, some men—" She broke off as applause erupted. "Look at them." She laughed, everything inside her warming as she watched Yuri and Nadia jitterbugging. "Aren't they great?"

"The best. Why don't we— Son of a bitch."

"What?" She blinked, then refocused. It appeared the lonely Ben and Lorelie were finding solace with each other. If *solace* was quite the word, Freddie mused, for the way they were nuzzling in the corner. "She's sitting in his lap."

"I see where she's sitting."

"So much for letting him down easy," Freddie muttered, just as Nick echoed the same sentiments, applied to Lorelie.

He snapped back first. "What? What did you say?"

"Nothing. I didn't say anything. What did you say?"

"Nothing."

Suddenly they were grinning at each other.

"Well..." Freddie let out a quick breath as her

fingers continued to move over the keys. "Don't they make a cute couple?"

"Adorable. Now they're going to dance."

"Too bad for her," Freddie said, with feeling. "Ben's a nice guy, but he dances like he's drilling for oil. I think he dislocated my shoulder."

"She can handle it. But let's slow this down before Yuri kills himself."

He segued into "Someone To Watch Over Me."

Freddie sighed, yearned. Romantic tunes always tugged at her heart. Flowing with it, she looked over at Nick. Maybe, while she was feeling so in tune with him, the taste of crow wouldn't stick in her throat.

"It was lovely, what you did for Grandma and Papa."

"No big deal. I just made a phone call, like you said."

"Truce," she murmured, and touched a hand to his for a moment. "It wasn't just the limo, Nick, though that was wonderful. Stocking it with all those white roses, caviar, iced vodka. It was very thoughtful."

"I figured they'd get a kick out of it." As usual, her simple sweetness layered guilt over his black mood.

Pass the crow.

"I came down pretty hard on you earlier. I should have taken into consideration all the time and effort you put into getting things ready for tonight and setting up your apartment. Though why it took you so long to look for a lamp is beyond me."

Her art deco lamp was her current pride and joy. "Why don't you stick with the apology?"

"You did a nice job on the party."

"Thanks." Pleased with the small victory, she signaled to her father to take over for her. "And since you talk so sweet," she added, leaning over to give him a kiss, "I forgive you."

"I wasn't asking you—" But she was already up and gone. Nick scowled when Spence took his daughter's place. "Women."

"Couldn't have put it better myself. She's certainly grown into an attractive, independent one."

"She was a nice kid," Nick mused. "You shouldn't have let her grow up."

Spence noted, with a glance at Nick's face, that Natasha's theory on romance probably was on the mark. There was an ache around his heart. Spence supposed there always would be, at the idea of his little girl moving into her own separate life. But there was pride, as well.

Seamlessly he meshed with Nick on a Ray Charles classic.

"You know," he continued, "boys are already coming by the house, flirting with Katie."

"No way." Shock raced into Nick's eyes first, then the uncomfortable feeling of, at thirty, actually beginning to feel old. "No way. If I had a daughter, no way I'd let that happen."

"Reality's tough," Spence agreed, then let the devil take over. "You know, Nick, it certainly eases my mind to know that you're around to look after

Freddie. I'd worry a lot more if I didn't have someone I trusted keeping an eye out.''

"Yeah." Nick cleared his throat. "Right. Listen, I'd better take over at the bar for a while.''

Spence grinned to himself and added a flourish to the notes.

"You shouldn't tease him," Natasha said from behind him, laying a hand on her husband's shoulder.

"It's my job, as a father, to make his life a living hell. And just think, with the practice I have, how good I'll be at it when it's Katie's turn.''

"I shudder to think.''

It was after two before the party broke. Now only Nick and Freddie and a few straggling family members remained. With a satisfied look, Freddie glanced around the bar.

It looked as though an invading army had suddenly pulled up stakes and gone off to another battle.

Tattered crepe paper hung drunkenly, so that white doves flew at half-mast. The tables that had been loaded with food had been thoroughly decimated, and all that was left of Rio's pièce de résistance, the five-tiered wedding cake, were crumbs and a few smears of silvery icing.

There were glasses everywhere. Some enterprising soul had built a fairly impressive pyramid of lowball glasses in the corner. She saw a forest of crumpled napkins littering the floor, and, oddly, a single gold shoe with a stiletto heel.

She wondered how its owner had managed to walk out without lurching.

Leaning against the bar, Zack took his own survey and grinned. "Looks like everybody had a good time."

"I'll say." Rachel picked up a cloth and gave the bar a halfhearted swipe. "Papa was still dancing on his way out, and my ears are ringing from Ukrainian folk songs."

"You belted out a few yourself," Zack reminded her.

"Vodka does that to me. Wasn't it wonderful, seeing their faces when we gave them their gift?"

"Grandma just cried," Freddie murmured.

"And Papa stood there telling her not to," Nick put in. "While he was crying himself."

"It was a wonderful idea, Freddie." Rachel's eyes filled again as she thought of it. "Lovely, romantic. Perfect."

"I knew we wanted to give them something special. I'd never have thought of it if Mama hadn't mentioned it."

"You couldn't have come up with better." Rolling her weary shoulders, Rachel took another look around. "Look, I vote we leave this mess and tackle it in the morning."

"I'm with you." More than willing to turn his back on the destruction, Zack took her hand and drew her around the bar. "Abandon ship."

"You two go ahead," Freddie said casually. She didn't want the night to end. And if prolonging it meant dealing with dirty dishes, so be it. "I just want to make a dent."

Guilt had Rachel hesitating. "I suppose we could—"

"No." Freddie aimed a quiet, meaningful look. "Go home. You've got a baby-sitter to deal with. I don't."

"Another hour won't matter," Zack said, squaring his shoulders.

"But we'll leave it to you," Rachel said, stepping hard on her husband's foot.

"But—"

Zack finally caught the drift, and the ensuing kick in the shin. "Oh, right. You kids get a start on it. I'm exhausted. Can hardly keep my eyes open." To add emphasis, he tried an exaggerated yawn. "We'll finish up what you don't tomorrow. Night, Freddie." Not sure if he should wink or issue a sharp warning in Nick's direction, Zack merely stared. "Nick."

"Yeah, see you." After the door closed, Nick shook his head. "He was acting weird."

"He was just tired," Freddie said as she loaded glasses onto a tray.

"No, there's tired and there's weird. That was weird." Which, Nick realized, was pretty much how he felt, now that he and Freddie were alone. "Listen, they've got the right idea. It's late. Why don't we pretend this is done, and go away? It'll still be here tomorrow."

"Go on up if you're tired." Freddie marched toward the kitchen with her loaded tray. "I couldn't sleep knowing I'd left all this. Not that it would bother you," she said over her shoulder as the door swung behind her.

"It's not like I made this mess myself," Nick muttered, loading another tray. "I think I spotted one or two other people using glasses around here tonight."

"Did you say something?" Freddie called out.

"No. Nothing."

He carted his tray into the kitchen, where she was already filling the dishwasher, and set it down with a clatter.

"You don't go to hell for leaving dishes in the sink."

"You don't win any prizes, either. I said go on up to bed. I can handle it."

"I can handle it," he mimicked in a mumble as he dragged out a pail. He stuck it in the sink, added a hefty dose of cleaner and a hard spray of hot water.

When he stalked out moments later, she was grinning.

For the next twenty minutes, they worked in silence that became more and more companionable. It pleased her to see the food cleared away, the bar gleaming again. And, she thought, while Nick wasn't exactly whistling while he worked, his mood was definitely clearing up.

"I noticed that Ben and Lorelie left together," Freddie began.

"You don't miss much." But his lips twitched. "They had a fine old time. Everybody did."

"You're not upset."

He shrugged. "It wasn't serious. Lorelie and I

never..." Whoops, watch your step. "We just didn't click."

She couldn't prevent the overwhelming sense of glee, but she did manage to conceal it. Humming a little, she picked up a chair, upended it onto a table in the area Nick had already mopped.

He swabbed a bit closer. Since she was being so easy about things, he thought it was time to clear the decks.

"Fred, I wanted to talk to you about this afternoon."

"All right. You know, if we clean up any more, Zack will think we don't need him. I don't want to hurt his feelings."

But she wandered over to the jukebox, loitered over the choices. Inspired, she pushed buttons, turned. "You didn't dance with me tonight, Nick."

"Didn't I?" He knew very well he hadn't, and why.

"No." She walked to him as the slow, shuffling notes seeped out. "If I Didn't Care," she thought. The Platters.

Perfect.

"You don't want to hurt my feelings, do you, Nicholas?"

"No, but—"

But she was already slipping her arms around him. He laid his hand on the small of her back and led her into the dance.

His movements were smooth and surprisingly stylish. Always had been, she remembered as she rested her head on his shoulder. The first time she danced with him, she'd thrilled to them.

But there was a different kind of thrill now, for the woman, rather than the adolescent girl.

She fit so well, he thought. Always had, he remembered as he drew her closer. But she'd never smelled like this before, and he couldn't remember her hair teasing him into brushing his lips over it.

They were alone, and the music was right. He'd always been susceptible to music. It tempted him now to rub his lips over her temple, nibble lightly at her ear.

Catching himself, he swung her out in a slow spin that made her laugh. Her eyes were glowing when she turned back into his arms.

She followed his every move as though she'd been born in his arms. Seemed to anticipate him as he walked her, circled her, twirled her again. In a move as gracefully choreographed as the dance, she lifted her head.

And his mouth was waiting.

He simply slid into her. Into the kiss, the warmth, the simplicity of it. Her arms came up, encircled his neck, her fingers skimming up threading into his hair.

He didn't hear the music end, for it was playing in his head. Their own intimate symphony. He thought he could absorb her if she would let him. Her skin, her scent, that wonderfully generous mouth.

As the kiss deepened, lengthened, he imagined

how perfectly simple it would be to pick her up, carry her upstairs. To his bed.

The clarity of the vision shocked him enough to have him pulling her back. "Fred—"

"No, don't talk." Her eyes were clouded, dreamily. "Just kiss me, Nick. Just kiss me."

Her mouth was on his again, making him long to forget all the reasons why it shouldn't be. However confused those reasons were becoming, he put his hands firmly on her shoulders and stepped back.

"We're not doing this."

"Why?"

"You're on dangerous ground here," he warned her. "Now get your things, your purse, whatever. I'm taking you home."

"I want to stay here, with you." Her voice was calm, even if her pulse rate wasn't. "I want to go upstairs with you, to bed."

The knot in his stomach tightened like a noose. "I said get your purse. It's late."

Her experience might be limited, but she thought she knew when to advance and when to retreat. On legs that weren't quite steady, she walked behind the bar to get her purse.

"Fine. We'll play it your way. But you don't know what you're missing."

Afraid he did, he dragged a hand through his hair. "Where did you learn this stuff?"

"I pick it up as I go along," she said over her shoulder as she yanked open the door. "Coming?"

It had just occurred to him that it might be a better—safer—idea to get her a cab. But she was already outside.

"Just hold on." He slammed the bar door behind him and locked it.

Freddie began to stroll down the street. "Beautiful night."

Nick muffled his muttering and methodical cursing. "Yeah, just dandy. Give me your purse."

"What?"

"Just give it to me." He snatched the glittery fancy and shoved it into his jacket pocket. For the first time, he noticed her earrings. "I bet those rocks are real."

"These?" Automatically she lifted a hand to the sapphire-and-diamond clusters. "Yes, why?"

"You should know better than to walk around with a year's rent on your earlobes."

"It's no use having them if I'm not going to wear them," she pointed out with perfect logic.

"There's a time and a place. And walking on the Lower East Side at 3:00 a.m. doesn't qualify for either."

"Want to put them in your pocket, too?" Freddie said dryly.

Before he could tell her it was just what he had in mind, someone called his name.

"Yo, Nick!"

Glancing across the deserted street, Nick saw the shadow, recognized it. "Just keep walking," he told Freddie, automatically shifting her to his far side. "And don't say anything."

Breathless from the short jog, a thin-faced man in

baggy pants fell into step beside them. "So, Nick, how's it hanging?"

"Can't complain, Jack."

Freddie opened her mouth, but only a muffled squeak came out when Nick crushed all the major bones of her hand.

"Fancy stuff." Jack winked at Nick and gave him an elbow dig. "You always had the luck."

The man was too pitiful to bother decking. "Yeah, I'm loaded with it. We've got places to go, Jack."

"Bet. Thing is, Nick, I'm short until payday."

When wasn't he? Nick thought. "Come by the bar tomorrow, I'll float you."

"Appreciate it. Thing is, I'm short now."

Still walking, Nick dug into his pocket, pulled out a twenty. He knew exactly where it would go, if Jack could link up with his dealer at this hour.

"Thanks, bro." The bill disappeared into the baggy pants. "I'll get it back to you."

"Sure." When icicles drip in hell. "See you around, Jack."

"Bet. Once a Cobra, always a Cobra."

Not, Nick thought, if he could help it. Furious at being forced into the encounter, and that Freddie had been touched by the slimy edge of his past, he quickened his pace.

"You know him from the gang you used to belong to," Freddie said quietly.

"That's right. Now he's a junkie."

"Nick—"

"He hangs around the neighborhood, sometimes

during the day. Odds are he won't remember you, he was already buzzed, but if you run into him, just keep running. He's bad news.''

''All right.'' She would have reached for him, tried to comfort him somehow, drive away the misery lurking just behind his eyes. But they had reached her building, and he was pulling her purse out of his pocket.

Nick took out her keys himself and unlocked the front door, then stepped inside and pressed the button for the elevator. ''Go upstairs. Lock your door.''

''Come up with me. Stay with me.''

He wanted to touch her, just once more. But his fingers still felt soiled where they had brushed Jack's over a crumpled twenty-dollar bill.

''Do you have any idea what happened just now?'' Nick demanded. ''We just ran into part of my life, and if I hadn't been along, he would have taken more from you than your pretty earrings.''

''He isn't part of your life,'' she said calmly. ''He isn't your friend. But you gave him money.''

''So maybe he won't mug the next person he sees.''

''You're not one of them anymore, Nick. I doubt you ever really were.''

He was suddenly so weary, so horribly tired. Giving in, he rested his brow against hers. ''You don't know what I was, what I still might be. Now go upstairs, Fred.''

''Nick—''

To silence her, he gripped her shoulders and brought his mouth down hard on hers. When she could breathe again, she would have staggered, but his hands steadied her as he pushed her into the elevator. She could only stare, system sizzling, as he snapped the grate closed.

''Lock your door,'' he said again, and walked out.

He took a careful look up the street, down, then turned and waited until he saw her light flash on.

He took the long way home.

Chapter Eight

She'd had incredible dreams. True, she'd gotten only a few hours' sleep, but she saw no reason to complain. In fact, Freddie had awakened early, feeling wonderful. Since she had time to spare, she walked over to the Village and spent the morning haunting some of the more interesting shops, picking up what Nick liked to call her knickknacks.

By the time she'd cabbed home, dropped off her newest treasures and walked out again, she was running a little behind.

But the day was too gorgeous for her to worry about it.

Spring was in full swing now, with just a hint of the summer to come teasing the edges. It made the day balmy and bright, with none of the horrendous heat that could plague the city during the dog days.

She was, Freddie decided, one of the luckiest women in the world. She lived in an exciting city, was embarking on a new, equally exciting career. She was young and in love. And, unless her female intuition was faulty, she was very close to convincing the man she loved that he loved her right back.

Every step of her plan was falling into place.

Since she was feeling generous, she stopped by a sidewalk vendor to buy both herself and Nick a jumbo pretzel.

As she was slipping her change back into her pocket, she spotted the man leaning on the front of the building across the street.

The thin face, the baggy clothes. With a little inward shiver, she recognized the man Nick had called Jack from the night before. He was smoking, bringing a cigarette to his lips in quick, greedy puffs as his eyes darted right and left like wary birds.

Even though those eyes lingered a moment on her before passing on, she saw no recognition in them. Relieved, she turned away. Not that she would have spoken to him unless it was unavoidable, Freddie thought. Still, she wouldn't have cared to explain to Nick about any interaction she had with one of his old gang comrades.

She quickened her pace, heading toward the bar without looking back. Though the back of her neck prickled.

She pushed Jack out of her mind as she stepped into the kitchen, and loitered there a few moments to praise Rio for his success with last night's food.

Nibbling on her pretzel, she started upstairs. Her

sunny mood didn't cloud over, even when Nick yanked open the door and scowled at her.

"You're late."

So much, she thought, for loverlike greetings.

"I wasn't even sure you'd be up yet. We had a late night."

He didn't care to be reminded of it. "I'm up, and I'm working, which is more than I can say for you."

He'd had much worse than a late night. He hadn't slept more than an hour, and even that had been restless and sweaty. Old dreams and new ones had plagued him.

He'd been raw then, and he was raw now, suffering from a combination of emotional and physical frustration he'd never experienced before.

And he knew just where to lay the blame for it.

She was standing right in front of him, looking as bright and golden as a sunbeam.

Though she was well aware of his foul mood, Freddie smiled at him, tilted her head. He hadn't bothered to shave, she noted, but she didn't object to the look. The angry eyes and stubbled chin gave him a sort of reckless and dangerous edge that was appealing, in its way.

She had a feeling he'd had trouble sleeping, and couldn't have been happier.

"Rough night, Nick? Have a pretzel."

Since she all but shoved it into his mouth, he had little choice but to take a bite. But he didn't have to like it.

"Where's the mustard?"

"Get your own." She crossed to the piano and sat. "Ready to work?"

"I've been working." What else was there to do, when you couldn't sleep? "What have you been doing?"

"Shopping."

"Figures."

"And before you start hammering me, I happened to have finished the lyrics to 'You're Not Here.'" Pleased to be able to put him in his place, she opened her briefcase and pulled them out. "I polished them up before the shops opened."

He muttered something, but joined her on the bench. In spite of himself, his mood began to lift as he read them. He should have known they'd be perfect.

Still, there was no use indulging her vanity. "They're not too bad."

She rolled her eyes. "Thank you, Richard Rodgers."

His mouth quirked. "You're welcome, Stephen Sondheim."

Now that he looked at her, really looked, his gaze narrowed. "What did you do to your hair?"

Instinctively she reached up to pat it. "I pulled it back and put it up. It gets in the way."

"I like it in the way." To prove it, he started yanking out pins.

"Stop it." Flustered, she batted at his hands. He simply caught her wrists, bracketing them with one hand while he used the other to pull her careful hairdo apart.

By the time the damage was to his liking, he was laughing and she was swearing at him. "There," he decided. "Much better."

"Now you're a fashion consultant."

"You look cute when it sort of sproings all over the place."

She blew it out of her face. "Sproings. Thanks." Now her eyes gleamed. "Maybe I'll do some rearranging on yours."

She made her dive, but he was quicker. It had always been a disappointment to her that she couldn't quite outmaneuver him. He just wrestled her backward until she was breathless and giggling.

It took her a moment to realize he wasn't smiling anymore, but was staring at her. Staring with a sharp, focused intensity that had her pulse stuttering and her throat going dry. Her legs had gotten tangled with his, so that she was all but sitting on his lap.

A tug, a sweet, gradual pull, stretched from her heart down to her center.

"Nick."

"We're wasting time." He let his hands fall away, untangled himself. He just had to get on the right track, he was sure of it, and he'd stop having these sudden, voracious cravings for her. "We'll run through the number you just finished, see how it plays."

Patience, she reminded herself, and wiped her damp palms on her trousers. "Fine. Whenever you're ready."

After a rocky start, the work smoothed out. Both

of them became focused on the music, so that they could sit hip to hip as collaborators, as friends.

One hour passed into two, and two into three, and more. At one point, Rio brought up some leftovers from the party, and stayed awhile to listen, with a smile on his wide face.

They nibbled at food, polished, argued over small points and nearly always agreed on the big ones.

Nearly.

"It should be romantic."

"Comedic," Nick disagreed.

"It's their wedding night."

"Exactly." He took time out for a cigarette, secretly pleased that he was cutting down on his tobacco intake daily. "They've rushed headlong into marriage. They've known each other three days."

"They're in love."

"They don't know what they are." Thoughtfully, he took a slow drag, setting the scene in his head. "They've just rushed off to a JP for a ridiculous ceremony, now they're in a broken-down hotel room, wondering what they've gotten into. And what the hell they're going to do about it."

"That may be, but it's still their wedding night. You're writing a dirge."

He only grinned. "Ever really listened to the Wedding March, Fred?" To prove his point, he crushed the cigarette out and began to play it.

Freddie had to admit it was solemn, serious, and a little scary. "Okay, you've got a point. Play it again and let me think."

She got up to pace, letting Nick's music run through her. And she watched him, and wondered.

What was it about him that pulled her so? His looks? Perhaps that had been true years ago, when a young girl first saw those restless green eyes. But she looked deeper now.

His manner? That made her smile. Hardly that. However kind and loving Nick could be, he could be equally brusque and careless of feelings. Not that he meant to hurt others' feelings, she thought. He simply forgot about them.

It was his heart, she decided, that had always called to hers, and always would.

But what if she had met him only yesterday? What if they had come together as strangers and she had simply, irrevocably lost that heart to him?

Would she be frightened, unsure? Excited?

"Who is this man," she murmured, "who calls me his wife? It takes more than a gold ring to change a girl's life."

She wrinkled her nose when Nick glanced back. "Needs to be sharper," she said.

Thinking, she took another turn around the room. "Till death do us part? That's a deal with no heart. Love, honor and cherish, from now till I perish?"

He turned and grinned. "I like it. Marriage and death. Quite a pair."

"I can do better. Who is this man, waiting outside the door? What's he want me to be? A wife, a lover, a whore? He's going to see me naked. There's no way I can fake it..."

She stopped, laughed, rubbed the back of her neck. "I'm getting punchy."

"It's the right theme," he told her. "Panic."

"Maybe...maybe." She walked back to him. "What if we started out the way you have it, slow, funereal—a cello-and-organ thing. Then we pick up the tempo, faster, then faster. Panic building."

"With a key change."

"Good. Try here." To demonstrate, she leaned over his shoulder, putting her hands over his on the keys.

"Yeah, I got the picture." He wished to God her breasts weren't pressing into his back. "You're crowding me, Fred."

The strain in his voice alerted her. "Am I? Sorry." But she wasn't, not a bit. She eased back a little, listening to him work. "I think we've got it." Gently she laid her hands on his shoulders and began to rub. "You're tight."

His fingers fumbled, infuriated him. "You're still crowding me."

"I know."

Her hair brushed his cheek, and that damned perfume she wore shot straight to his loins. Intending on snarling at her, he turned his head—his first mistake—and ended up staring into those wide gray eyes.

"Am I making you nervous, Nicholas?" she murmured, as she slid onto the stool beside him.

The simple truth came out before he could stop it. "You're making me crazy."

"Good." She leaned forward, and pressed a soft,

lascivious kiss with just a hint of tongue full on his lips before he could evade. "You've been making me crazy for years. It's about time I had a turn."

His breath was backing up in his lungs. He thought he understood exactly how a man feels when he goes down for the third time. Choking, floundering. And fighting a losing battle with fate.

His voice hardened in defense. "This isn't a game, Fred, and you don't know the rules."

She slid her hands up his forearms, rested them on his shoulders, then moved in slowly, until her mouth was nearly on his. "I imagine you could teach me."

He was holding on to control by a thread, a slippery, frayed thread that kept dancing out of his hands. "If you knew what I'd like to teach you, you'd run, and run fast, all the way home to Daddy."

That statement had pride kicking in. Her chin shot up, and her eyes dared him. "Try me."

It was insane, he knew it was insane, to drag her against him, to plunder that teasing, tormenting mouth with his. He told himself he'd wanted to frighten her, to make her leap up and race for the door, for her own good.

But it was a lie.

When her body quivered against his, then strained, then melted, that thin thread snapped and sent him tumbling.

"Damn it. Damn both of us." He dragged her off the stool, caught her up in his arms in a gesture every woman dreams of. "You're not walking away this time."

Her breath might have come in shallow gasps, but she met his eyes levelly. "I'm not the one that's been walking away, Nick. And you're not going to get me to run, either."

"Then God help you. God help us both."

His mouth was on hers again, wild and free, as he whirled her into the bedroom.

The sheets were in tangles on the unmade bed, a testament to his restless night. The late-afternoon sun beat on the windows so that the light was harsh and unforgiving. Another time, he might have given some thought to ambience, to the romantic trappings she might have hoped for.

But now he simply fell with her onto the bed, and plundered.

His hands were already dragging at her blouse, and his lips were everywhere. She didn't protest the speed, or the urgency, but met it, beat for beat. After waiting for him for so long, it seemed right to hurry. Perhaps there was a small seed of panic lodged inside her. The fear that she would fumble when it counted most.

Would there be pain? she wondered. Humiliation?

Then his mouth was hot on hers again, and the seed died, withered by the heat, before it had the chance to grow.

She'd never imagined it could be like this. So violent and intense a need. So exciting. All her fantasies, her long-held dreams and quiet hopes, paled against the brilliance of reality.

He couldn't get enough of her. It seemed as if he'd waited all his life for this one moment. She was a banquet of flavors, tart, sweet, tangy, and he a starving man.

Her skin was ivory-pale, with a fire just underneath that seduced and enraptured. Each small movement she made, as fluid as the dance they'd shared the night before, aroused him beyond belief.

Part of his brain understood that she was innocent. He knew she was small, delicate. He could feel that fragile skin, those subtle curves, under his hands. So without even realizing it, he slowed his pace. And began to savor.

There was sweetness in her. The shape of her mouth, the curve of her shoulder. Gently he skimmed his lips down her throat, calling on patience now to allow her to adjust to each new level of pleasure. So he played her with care, with skill. Adding notes and small flourishes, letting them linger, sustain. And as he felt each response shiver through her, saw it mirrored on her face, he found there was no need to hurry after all.

She couldn't keep her eyes open. They were too heavy. Odd, how light the rest of her felt. Like thin, fragile glass. And he stroked and cupped her in those wonderful artist's hands, as if he knew she might break.

Then his mouth moved down, circling, teasing, then capturing, her breast. The pleasure arrowed into her and quivered there.

To touch him, she thought hazily. At last to touch him. To feel that wiry strength, those muscles covered by taut skin. Murmuring her approval, she ran her hands over him freely, delighted with each new discovery.

Those soft, testing caresses had the blood pounding in his head. When his mouth came back to hers again, he demanded just a little more—just a little deeper, a little longer.

He thought she looked like a princess under glass, with her eyes closed, her skin glowing and her hair like a sunburst over his pillow.

But she was trembling beneath him, her lips were full and swollen from his patient, relentless assault, and her breath was quickening. Focused on her, only her, he eased her gently toward the next level.

When he cupped her, she was hot and wet and irresistible.

Her eyes flew open at the new intimacy. And the pressure, the unbearable pressure that seemed to press outward through her body, threatening to shatter her, promising to overwhelm. Even as she shook her head in denial, she arched against him.

He took her flying toward the first peak so that she cried out, shocked, staggered by the impact. Her nails bit heedlessly into his back in response to the violence that gripped her, held her helpless. And made her crave.

Then the tension spurted out of her, leaving her limp. She thought she heard him groan, felt him shudder even as she shuddered. But he was taking her high again, so quickly, so skillfully, that she could only cling and let him lead.

His hands were balled into fists as he eased himself into her, slowly, so slowly that sweat sprang to his skin and his body seemed to scream out for release.

He knew he would hurt her. Damage her. Invade her.

But she opened for him fluidly, as if she'd been waiting all along.

He would burn in hell for what he'd done. Nick cursed himself over and over, but he couldn't find the strength to move. He was still sprawled over her, still inside her, trying to recover from the climax of his life.

He'd had no right to take her. Less to find any pleasure in it.

He wished she would say something, anything, so that he would have some clue to how to handle the situation. But she only lay there, limply, with one hand resting lightly on his back.

His responsibility, he reminded himself. And it was time to face the music.

As gently as possible, he shifted, rolled off her. She made some sound, vaguely feline, as he moved, then simply curled to him.

He would certainly burn in hell, he thought, for wanting her all over again.

"There's nothing I can do to make up for this."

"Nothing," she said with a sigh, and rested her hand on the old scar above his heart.

He stared fiercely at a spot on the ceiling. "Can I get you something? Brandy, maybe?"

"Brandy?" Puzzled, she drummed up enough energy to move her head and look at him. "I haven't been in an accident or been caught in an avalanche. Why would I need brandy?"

"For the...shock," he supposed. "Water, then," he said, disgusted with himself. "Something."

The lovely pink mists were clearing from her brain. Clearing enough that she could see the regret and self-condemnation in his eyes. "You're not going to tell me you're sorry this happened."

"Damned right I'm sorry, for whatever good it does. I should never have touched you. Never have let things get this far. I knew it was your first time."

Pride wobbled. "How?"

He finally shot her a look. "Let's just say it was obvious."

"I see." Perhaps, after such stunning pleasure, there could be humiliation. "Was I inadequate?"

"In—" He let out a breath, then a curse. The woman had turned him inside out, now she wanted to know if she was inadequate. "No, you weren't inadequate. You were amazing."

"I was?" Her lips began to curve. "Amazing?"

He recognized that smug tone and wondered how, at such a time, it could amuse him. "That's not the point."

"I think it's a good one, though." Understanding, and sorry for the torment she heard in his voice, she shifted until she could look down at his face. "I always knew you'd be my first, Nicholas. I always wanted you to be."

He wondered why the thrill that sent through him didn't shame him. "I took advantage—"

She cut him off with a delighted laugh. "No way.

Maybe you want to delude yourself that you ravished the virgin, Nicholas, but I seduced you, and I worked damned hard at it.''

"I'm trying to take responsibility here," he said patiently. "You're making it tough."

"You made me happy," she murmured, and lowered her mouth lightly to his. "I hope we made each other happy. Why should knowing that make you sad?"

It didn't seem to make much sense, but he found himself smiling at her. "You're supposed to be weepy and trembling and shocked."

"Oh." She pursed her lips. "Well, maybe if we take it from the top—so to speak—I'll get it right the next time."

Later, he left her in his bed and went down to the bar for his shift. For the first time in years, he caught himself watching the clock. Though he drew drafts and mixed drinks with the ease of experience, he nearly snarled at the few customers who lingered through last call.

The minute the last one was out the door, he locked up. He gave the bar no more than a cursory cleanup before rushing back upstairs.

She was sleeping, her head nestled in his pillow, her arm thrown out over the space where he would soon be. He found himself grinning, delighted just to watch her, to listen to the slow, even sound of her breathing, the little catch in it when she shifted in sleep and rustled the sheet.

Then an idea began to form in his brain that had him grinning and unbuttoning his shirt.

He left his clothes in a heap on the floor, then eased down at the edge of the bed. He tugged the sheet aside and picked up her foot.

Freddie drifted awake on a tingle of pleasure. It seemed to creep along her skin, seep into her blood. She heard herself sigh with it, a lovely dream. Then she shot fully awake and into a sitting position when Nick scraped his teeth along her instep.

"Nick?" Disoriented, pulse pumping, she pushed the hair out of her eyes and blinked at the shadow at the bottom of the bed. "What are you doing?"

"Waking you up."

His eyes, well adjusted to the dark, gleamed like a cat's. A wolf's. He found it endearing, arousing, that when she discovered she had no sheet to cover herself, she crossed an arm over her breasts and looked flustered.

"Too late," he murmured. "I've already seen you naked."

Feeling foolish, she lowered her arm. A little.

"I had this interesting fantasy, about nibbling on your toes and working my way up. I'm indulging myself."

"Oh." The idea had heat rushing through her. "Come to bed."

"Eventually."

"I want to…" She trailed off, sliding bonelessly back down as his tongue did amazing and wicked things to her ankle.

"I figured since you seduced me—" he progressed, inch by devastating inch, up her calf "—it was only right that I return the favor."

Who would have thought, she wondered, that the

back of a knee could be so wonderfully sensitive? "Well..." Her voice was weak. "Fair's fair."

When Freddie let herself into her apartment the next morning, she was singing. Not only was she in love, she thought, but Nick LeBeck was her lover. And she was his.

She did three quick pirouettes across her living room, buried her face in the tiny white blooms of the violet he'd given her, then spun away again.

Everything in her life was suddenly and absolutely perfect.

She would have deserted her beautiful new apartment and moved into the pigsty he lived in in an instant, bag and baggage. But she could easily imagine Nick's face if she brought up the idea.

Total shock, she acknowledged. And a good dose of fear.

Well, there was no need to rush, she reminded herself. Not now.

But if he didn't make a move before too much longer, she would have to take the initiative herself. And propose.

Still, at the moment, she was more than content. All she wanted was a shower—the one she'd taken with Nick that morning didn't count—and a change of clothes. She was due back at Nick's in an hour.

They still had a score to finish.

She was just stepping, dripping, out of the shower when her buzzer sounded.

"Coming, coming, coming." Tugging on a robe as she ran, she rushed to the intercom. "Yes?"

"Fred, open up."

The sound of his voice still had the power to thrill her. "Nick, you've got to stop following me."

"Ha-ha. Now open up. I wouldn't have had to run all the way over here if you'd answered your phone."

"I was in the shower." She pressed the buzzer to admit him, then undid her locks before dashing back to the bathroom. She managed to tuck her hair into a towel, and slather on some moisturizer before he walked in.

"Don't *ever* leave your door unlocked like that."

Always the sweet-talker, she thought. "You were on your way up."

"Ever," he repeated, then eyed her. "Didn't you just take a shower an hour ago?"

She tilted her head, then shoved the towel back into place as it tipped. "I put that more in the class of water games than grooming. What are you, the water police?"

Distracted, he reached out to toy with her lapel. "What do you call this thing?"

She glanced down at her short plum-colored silk robe. "A robe. What do you call it?"

"An invitation, but we haven't got time. Get packed."

Her brows shot up. "I'm leaving?"

"We're leaving. Maddy O'Hurley called five minutes after you left. She wants us to come to her house for a few days up at the Hamptons. In the Hamptons. Whatever."

Since the towel refused to stay in place, Freddie pulled it off. "Now?"

"That's the idea. Her weekend home's there, and

she's got the family with her." Idly he reached out and tugged one of her wet curls. "She thought it would be an opportunity for us to work together, and have a little R and R while we're at it."

"Sounds like a plan."

"So hurry up, will you?" Impatience was shimmering around him now. "I've got to get back and do my own packing, rent a car and arrange for someone to take over my shift at the bar."

"Okay, go get busy. I'll be ready when you are."

"You wouldn't want to put any money on it, would you? Holy hell!" He'd backed into the bedroom as he spoke, and now stood gaping. "What is that?"

"A bed," she told him, stepping forward to run a loving hand over the curved footboard. "My bed. Fabulous, isn't it?"

He grinned. "Arabian Nights or Sleeping Beauty. I can't decide which."

"Something in between." She arched a brow. "It's bigger than yours."

"It would make three of mine." He fingered the lace of the spread. He would have banked on her choosing lace. Slowly, he turned his head, looked back at her with a gleam in his eyes, and lust in his heart. "So, Fred, just how fast can you pack?"

"Fast enough," she promised, and leaped onto the bed with him.

Chapter Nine

Freddie didn't see why she couldn't drive. The snappy convertible Nick had rented for the trip was a pleasure, and she enjoyed having the wind rush through her hair, the blast of the radio. But she'd have preferred being behind the wheel.

"How come you get to drive?" she demanded.

"Because I've driven with you, Fred. You poke."

"I do not poke. I simply obey the law."

"Poke." Enjoying himself, he increased the pressure on the gas pedal. There was nothing like driving full-out with Ray Charles pumping out of the stereo. "If you were driving, we wouldn't get there until next week."

"You've already managed to get one ticket," she reminded him primly.

Ten miles out of the city, Nick thought in disgust,

and he'd been busted. "Traffic cops have no sense of adventure." But Nick did, and proved it by taking a turn fast. "This baby handles," he murmured. "Okay, navigator, check when our next turn's coming. I think we're almost on it."

Freddie glanced down at the directions, snickered. "You passed it, hotshot, about a half a mile back."

"No problem." He zipped the car into a tight U-turn that had Freddie caught between a scream and laughter.

"The general population can sleep easy, knowing you live in Manhattan and don't own a car. Make a left," she instructed. "And slow down. I'd like to get there in one piece."

He eased back—a little—and scanned the big, rambling houses they passed. Lots of lawn, he mused, lots of glass. Lots of money.

Big rooms, he imagined, filled with Oriental rugs and pricey antiques. Or glossy floors and stunning modern furnishings. Swimming pools with sparkling water and cushy lounge chairs set around them.

Though, of course, those would be sheltered by trimmed shrubbery and grand old trees.

Just the sort of neighborhood he would have been barred from a decade or so before. Now, he was here by invitation.

"It's that one." Freddie leaned forward. "The cedar with the weeping cherries in the front. Oh, aren't they beautiful?"

The blossoms were just past their peak, already littering the ground with fragile pink petals, but they did make a show. Nick couldn't claim to know a lot about horticulture, but he thought the scent tickling his senses was lilac.

When he turned into the sloping driveway, he was rewarded by the sight of a majestic bush loaded with lavender-hued spikes.

"Not bad for a weekend getaway," he murmured, studying the multileveled structure of glass and wood. "It must have twenty rooms."

"Probably. I wonder if—" Freddie broke off as a horde of children raced around from the far side of the house. Though of varying sizes and shapes, they appeared as a mass.

Until a slim, dark-haired boy took another child out with a flying tackle that was likely to jar internal organs.

Taking the cue, the rest of them piled on, shouting and wrestling.

"I see Maddy meant it literally when she told you the family would be here. The whole family, from the looks of it," Freddie observed. "That's Maddy's oldest boy trying to murder one of Trace's kids. I think."

She smiled as a pixie-size girl with wild red curls and an unidentifiable smear on her cheek spotted them, and waved.

"Mom!" the girl shouted. "Hey, Mom, company." As an afterthought, she gave the cousin she held in a headlock one last jab in the ribs, then scrambled up and raced to the car.

"Hi, I'm Julia. Remember me?"

"Of course I do." After she'd climbed out of the car, Freddie gave Maddy's youngest daughter a welcoming kiss. "Nick, this is Julia Valentine. I won't try to sort the others out for you quite yet."

"Hi, Julia." She had the look of her mother, he thought. If Maddy O'Hurley really looked like the woman he'd seen on stage and on billboards. "You've got quite a war going on."

"Hi." Julia beamed a smile at him. "We like to fight. We're Irish."

Nick had to grin. "That accounts for it."

"There's a lot of us, 'cause most everybody had twins. Trace had *two* sets of twins. But Aunt Chantel had triplets." She wrinkled her nose. "All boys. Come in. I'll take you inside."

Being female, if only seven, Julia focused on Nick. "I'm going to be a dancer on Broadway. Like Mom. You can write my music."

"Thanks."

As Julia opened the door, they were greeted by a small, towheaded boy with a maniacal gleam in his eye and a croaking frog in his hands.

"Put Chauncy back, Aaron," Julia ordered, with the perfect disdain of older sibling for younger. "He doesn't scare anybody."

"He will when he gets teeth," Aaron said darkly, and scrambled out.

"That's my little brother. He's a pain."

Before anyone could comment, a red-haired rocket fired down the stairs. She was wearing ragged cutoff shorts, no shoes, and an oversize, faded T-shirt that claimed she loved New York.

Maddy O'Hurley, Broadway's baby, made her entrance with style.

"Aaron, you little beast. Where are you? Didn't I tell you to keep this lizard in the aquarium?"

Spotting her visitors, she screeched to a halt, holding a very annoyed-looking silvery reptile by the middle.

"Oh." She blew the hair out of her eyes. "So much for elegant entrances. Freddie." She started to leap forward for a hug, remembered, and held the lizard out to her daughter.

"Julia, do me a favor and put this thing back where it belongs." That disposed of, she caught Freddie in a hard embrace. "It's so good to see you. I'm glad you could come."

"So am I."

"And you're Nick." With an arm still around Freddie's shoulders, she held out a hand. "It's great to meet you, at last. I've admired your work for a long time."

Nick knew he was staring, and didn't care. She did look like the woman he'd seen on the stage, on billboards. Porcelain skin, expressive face. And despite being the mother of four, a dancer's gracefully athletic build.

"My first Broadway show," he said. "Ten, eleven years ago. You were headlining. I've never seen anything like you before, or since."

"Well." Maddy decided a handshake wasn't enough, and kissed him instead. "I'm going to like you. Let's go see who else is around. We can take your stuff upstairs later."

The house wandered and was full of light, from wide glass doors, bow windows, skylights. There were occasional obstacles—toy trucks, a baseball mitt, someone's disreputable sneakers. Those touches of home melded easily with the elegance of the architecture.

In a spacious sun room, decked with exotic flowers and lacy ferns, a Hollywood legend lounged.

Chantel O'Hurley had her feet up, and her eyes closed. Nearby stood a man whose tough build and stance shouted *cop* to Nick's well-schooled brain.

"Brent's holding his own," Quinn Doran said, watching the children through the glass. "He may be the runt of our litter, angel, but he's game."

"Monsters," Chantel murmured, but there was a mother's indulgence in the word. "Why, if I was going to have triplets, couldn't they have been nice, well-mannered little girls?"

"They'd have bored you to death. Besides, who showed them how to use a slingshot?"

She smiled to herself. Of course, she had. Her boys, she thought. Hers. After years of longing, being afraid to hope, she'd netted three at one time.

Lazily she held out a hand, the way a woman does when she knows it will always be taken. "Come over here, Quinn, before someone finds us."

"Too late," Maddy announced. "Company. Nick, my sister Chantel, doing her Cleopatra impression, and her husband, Quinn Doran."

"Freddie." Chantel shifted fluidly to kiss Freddie's cheek, but her gaze lifted to Nick. "What excellent taste you have, darling."

"I think so."

Now Nick wasn't just staring. He was goggling.

The blond goddess aimed her sizzling blue eyes at him and smiled. Every nerve ending in his body went on full alert.

"You're writing the score for Maddy's new musical. From what I'm told, you've enough talent to make her sound professional."

Maddy simply sniffed. "She's just jealous because I have two Tonys and she only has one measly Oscar." Satisfied, Maddy signaled. "Come on, we'll see who else we can find."

"Just a minute," Freddie murmured as she and Nick passed out of the room through the doorway. She dabbed lightly at the corner of his mouth.

"What is it?"

"Oh, nothing. Just a little drool."

"Funny." But he didn't resist one last look over his shoulder at the vision lounging on the floral chaise. "She's even better in person."

"Pull yourself together, Nicholas. I'd hate to have Quinn kill you in your sleep. Rumor is he'd know how to do it, quickly and quietly." Before he could comment, Freddie let out a shout. "Trace!"

While Nick watched, narrow-eyed, she launched herself into the well-muscled arms of a tawny man with a boxer's build.

"Freddie." Trace kissed her lavishly. "How's my pretty girl?"

"I'm fine." Slinging an arm around Trace's neck, she beamed back at Nick. "Trace O'Hurley, Nick LeBeck."

"Nice to meet you."

Though he was friendly enough, his eyes

skimmed over Nick in a way that shouted *cop* again. Odd, Nick mused, he'd thought the guy was a musician. He'd even admired his work. But a cop's eyes were a cop's eyes.

"Most everybody else is in the kitchen," Trace continued. "Abby's cooking."

"Thank God," Maddy put in. "She's the only one we can trust. Are you hungry?"

"Well, I—"

"You must be hungry." She linked an arm through Nick's and barreled on, before he could finish the thought. "I'm always frantic to eat after a trip."

She led the way down a zigzagging hall. Nick noted that Trace didn't bother to set Freddie back on her feet, but carried her along, like some kind of white knight with a damsel.

The noise reached them first, and then Maddy swung open a door.

The kitchen was huge, but so crowded with bodies and motion that it seemed cozy. Only the blond woman stirring something at the stove appeared at rest.

A scrawny man with thinning hair was whirling a middle-aged woman around the room. Their steps meshed almost magically, and they miraculously avoided—through some internal radar, Nick supposed—collisions with chairs, counters and onlookers.

"Then when we went into the last number," Frank announced as he spun Molly in three tight circles, "we brought the house down."

With impressive grace, he whipped his wife into the arms of the man leaning against the kitchen counter, then picked himself up a redhead.

"Molly knows I've got two left feet." Dylan Crosby chuckled and passed his mother-in-law to his oldest son. "Here, Ben, dance with your grandmother before I damage her."

Spotting Trace, Frank grinned widely. "I've got your wife, Tracey! The girl would have a career on the boards if she'd just give up science." He dipped Gillian fluidly, then spun her back. "Hi, there, Freddie girl."

Seamlessly Trace passed Freddie to Frank, so that she was caught up in surprisingly ropey arms and became part of the dance. "You dance, boy?" he shouted at Nick.

"Actually, I—"

"Dad, let them catch their breath." Chuckling, Abby turned from the stove and moved to Nick. "Welcome to bedlam. I'm Abby Crosby."

"You were an O'Hurley first," her father reminded her.

"Abby O'Hurley Crosby," she corrected. "And if you sit down quickly enough, Dad won't be able to make you learn to do a time step."

They were quite a crew, Nick discovered. Before he fell into his own extended family, he hadn't really believed people lived this way. But, like the Stanislaskis, this confusing, noisy group was a family.

And Nick had learned that such families often talked over each other, around each other, and very often through each other. They picked petty fights, argued over nothing, chose sides. And united like steel against any outside foe.

He knew he was going to enjoy them, could already tell some of the kids apart by the time the chaotic meal they shared was over. Twins and triplets abounded, just to confuse things. But it was no surprise, he supposed, as Maddy and her sisters were triplets themselves.

After the kitchen was cleared, both Freddie and Nick had agreed willingly with Maddy's suggestion that they run through a few numbers.

It didn't take long for Nick to adjust himself to the household's jumpy rhythm. They even managed to get a little work done between distractions.

"Mom." Maddy's oldest girl came to the music room doorway. "Douglas is being a jerk again." Cassandra's gaze was dark as she complained about her twin.

"He's just a male, honey," Maddy told her. "You have to be patient."

Reed shot his wife a bland look over her opinion of his species. "Cassie, your mother's working, remember?"

"I remember." Cassie heaved a sigh. "No interruptions unless there's blood. Maybe there will be," she muttered before moving off.

"Why don't we take it from the second verse?" Maddy suggested, obviously unconcerned about the possibility of fratricide. "Don't stop now. I've got places to go, people to see."

"From the diaphragm, Maddy," Frank instructed

as he strolled in three measures later. "You won't reach the back row that way. It's a nice tune," he told Nick and Freddie. "Had me whistling. In fact, I was thinking about the movements. You know, if we—"

"Dad, we really need to get the vocals before we worry about choreography. Where's Mom?" Maddy asked, before he could tell her why she was wrong.

"Oh, off with some of the kids. Now, I was thinking—"

"Probably went for ice cream." If her mother wasn't around to jerk his chain, Maddy knew, she had to resort to dirty tactics. "I heard a rumor about fudge ripple."

"Oh?" Frank's eyes glazed, then gleamed. "Well, then I'd better go find them. Can't have the children overindulging. Dentist's bills, you know."

"Sorry." Maddy lifted a hand as her father scooted out. "My family."

"No problem." Nick tried a new chord. "I've got one of my own. Second verse," he said, then lost every thought in his head as Chantel sauntered in.

"Oh, don't mind me," she purred. "I'll just sit over in the corner, quiet as a mouse."

"A rat," Maddy muttered. "Go away, Chantel, you're distracting my composer."

Amused that it was no less than the truth, Chantel shrugged her creamy shoulders. "Well, if you're going to be temperamental, I'll go out by the pool. Maybe some of the kids want to take a dip." She aimed a last melting smile at Nick, and glided away.

"Don't worry." Maddy patted Nick's shoulder as

he stared blankly at the keys. "She affects men that way. Testosterone poisoning."

"Second verse, Nick." Freddie helped the reminder along with an elbow to his ribs.

"Right, I was just…thinking."

He made the effort, managed to complete the verse, move into the chorus, but then Abby raced by the music room window, screaming with laughter as she was pursued by her husband with a very large water gun.

"The children," Reed said, and shook his head. "Why don't we consider this a successful day's work and take a break? A swim sounds like a good idea."

"A brilliant one," Maddy agreed.

"You go ahead." Freddie picked up a sheet of music. "I'd like to fiddle with this for a few minutes."

"Come out when you're done, then." Maddy reached for Reed's hand. "If you can face it."

Nick craned his neck to try to get a glimpse of the pool. "Do you think she'll wear a bikini?"

Freddie lifted a brow. "Maddy?"

They both knew who he'd meant, but the alternative wasn't an image a man would sneeze at, either. Seeing that Nick was lost in consideration of numerous bikini-clad O'Hurleys, Freddie laughed.

"Animal."

He ran his tongue over his teeth. "You think Abby's going swimming, too?"

"I think you can get in trouble ogling married women. Now, if you can get your hormones under control, I'd like to run through 'You're Not Here.' Maddy might like to work on it later."

"It's rough yet."

"I know, but the core's there."

True enough, he thought. And it might smooth out the edges if they could work on it with Maddy, face-to-face. "Okay. I was thinking, if we tried it this way..."

Freddie closed her eyes, listened as the first notes drifted out. Nodding to herself, she added her voice to his music.

On the patio, Maddy held up a hand, then laid it on Abby's shoulder. "Listen."

"It's lovely," Abby murmured as her eyes misted. "Sad and lovely. She doesn't hide it very well when she sings. Being in love with him."

"No." Chantel slipped an arm around Abby's waist, so that the three of them stood together. "I guess they'll muddle through it."

"We did." With the music floating over them, Maddy gazed out over the lawn, toward the pool.

There was Dylan, coaching one of Trace's girls in a back flip. And Chantel's triplets, in a heated lap race, with Gillian and Cassie playing referee. Douglas was being the jerk his twin considered him, splashing Trace's other daughter.

Her father sat, eating fudge ripple ice cream with Trace's twin boys on either knee.

Ben and Chris, the boys Abby had raised alone for a time, were tall, handsome young men, arguing about which cassette to put into the portable stereo.

Quinn and Trace sat in the shade, sharing a beer

and war stories, while Molly applauded Abby's only daughter, Eva, on her underwater somersaults.

Aaron and Abby's youngest boy searched the grass for anything with more than two legs. Julia turned cartwheels to annoy them.

My family, she thought as she lifted a hand to wave to Reed. All present and accounted for.

"I feel good." Maddy drew in a deep breath, threw her face back to the sun. "And I have a strong feeling that those two at the piano are going to help me cop another Tony."

Unable to resist, Chantel slid her gaze toward her sister. "Oh, darling, do you have one already?"

With a rollicking laugh, Chantel ran, with Maddy inches behind.

Late, late at night, when the house was finally quiet, Nick drew Freddie to him, so that her head rested on his shoulder. Since Maddy had been considerate enough to give them adjoining rooms, he'd felt no guilt about sneaking into Freddie's bed.

It was good to simply lie there, with his heartbeat leveling toward normal, and his body sated from the slow, quiet love they'd made. She felt so natural curled up against him, he wondered how he'd ever slept without her.

"Tired?" he asked her.

"Hmm. Relaxed. It's been a terrific day. I loved seeing all of them again, how much the kids have grown. Everything."

"They're quite a group."

"They are that. I think it's great the way they all

juggle their schedules so they can have a week or two each year with everyone in the same place. Sometimes they go to Dylan and Abby's farm in Virginia.'' She sighed sleepily and cuddled closer when his fingers began to stroke along her shoulder. ''We visited there once. It's beautiful, all rolling hills, horses grazing. Space.''

''You'd need a lot of room with all these kids. Abby has the twin girls, right?''

''No, that's Trace and Gillian. Abby has four— Ben, Chris, Eva and Jed. And she had them one at a time.''

''Four.'' He shuddered.

''You love kids.'' She shifted, turning her head so that she could study his face. It was beautiful in the splash of moonlight, dreamy and heroic, like something out of an Arthurian legend.

''Sure I do. But it always amazes me that some people can handle so many, want to handle so many.''

She was caught up in the way he looked, that cool, sculpted face, the sea-green eyes. The way it felt to press against him, warm, exciting and right.

''I like big families. I was an only child for a few years. I wasn't lonely, because Dad was always there. But everything just clicked into place when Natasha came into our lives. I wanted a baby sister,'' she remembered. ''But Brandon came first, and that suited me fine.''

Nick had been an only child himself. But he'd had no father to be there. ''I used to wish for a brother. Then I had Zack.'' He shrugged. ''He went to sea, and I didn't.''

Her generous heart ached for the boy he'd been. ''It was hard on you, his leaving.''

''He did what he had to do. At the time, it seemed like he was leaving me. Just me. I got over it.''

The wave of love rolled over her, making her careless with words. ''So now you have a brother again, and an enormous family. You never have to be alone, unless you want to. That's why I'd like at least three children myself.''

A little warning blip sounded in his brain. He glanced down at her, then focused carefully on the ceiling. ''Well.''

Succinctly put, Freddie thought, but she didn't allow herself to sigh. It was much too soon to think about children. Their children.

It was a good time, as Nick saw it, to change the subject. ''Chantel doesn't look like anyone's mother.''

Now Freddie lifted a brow. ''Well, she is. And, if you don't mind a little friendly advice, you really should try to keep your tongue from hanging out every time she walks into the room.''

He looked at her again, leered. ''Jealous?''

She surprised, and insulted, him by bursting into delighted laughter. It rocked her hard enough that she was forced to sit up and try, unsuccessfully, to catch her breath.

Looking down at his scowling face only started her up again.

''You're overdoing it,'' he complained.

"Jealous." Gasping for air, she pressed a hand to her stomach. "Oh, right, Nicholas. I'm green. No doubt she'd toss Quinn aside in a heartbeat to run off with you. Anyone can see they only tolerate each other. That's why the air starts to sizzle when they're in the same room together."

His pride was injured, a little. "So she's stuck on her husband. Anyway, how do you figure he handles those steamy love scenes she plays on the screen?"

"By knowing she's not playing a scene when she's with him, I imagine." Unable to resist, she brushed her fingers through his hair. "That's what marriage is all about, isn't it? Trust and respect, as well as love and passion?"

Another warning blip. "I suppose," he said, and let it stop there. "Zack's going to drop his teeth when I get back and tell him about meeting her. He's seen some of her movies enough times to recite the dialogue."

"So, you'll gloat."

"Damn right."

Relaxed again, he glanced down at her. She looked so pretty, so…magical, he supposed, in the streams of moonlight that poured through the skylight. Her hair was a mess, the way he liked it best, and her lips were barely curved, as if she were thinking of something that pleased her.

"Not tired, huh?"

More than interested, she walked her fingers up his chest. She had been thinking of something that pleased her. She'd been thinking of him.

"I wondered if you'd get back to that."

"Just building up my strength."

"Good." Laughing, she rolled on top of him. "'Cause you're going to need it."

Chapter Ten

"You're telling me you met Chantel O'Hurley. *The* Chantel O'Hurley."

"That's what I said." It was a big charge for Nick to pull one off on Zack. It was no secret that the blond goddess was one of "Zack's little fantasies," as Rachel dryly put it. "The same Chantel O'Hurley whose movies you buy on video the minute they hit the stands." He hefted another crate of club soda into the storeroom.

"Wait a minute. Just a minute." Going in behind Nick empty-handed, Zack tugged on his sleeve. "You mean you met her, in the flesh?"

"She's got some terrific flesh, too, let me tell you." It didn't hurt to gloat. "I had dinner with her, a couple of times." Nick made sure it sounded off-hand, added a shrug for good measure. "Of course, her sisters aren't chopped liver, either. They're both—''

''Yeah, yeah, we'll talk about her sisters later. You had dinner, I mean, like dinner? With her?'' Zack found he had to clear his throat. ''Together. With her.''

''That's right.'' Of course, the meal had been shared by an entire household, kids included, but there was no need to mention those small details. ''I told you I was going to spend a couple of days with Maddy and Reed.''

''I wasn't thinking,'' Zack muttered. ''Didn't put it together. If you really met her, had dinner with her, what's she like?''

Nick turned, pursed his lips in an exaggerated kiss.

''Come on, you're killing me.'' A victim of his own fantasies, Zack hurried out after Nick. ''I mean, how does she look, just hanging around?''

''She filled out her bikini just fine.''

''Bikini.'' Overcome, Zack pressed a hand to his heart. ''You saw her in a bikini.''

''We took a couple swims together, sure.'' Actually, he and Freddie had been entertaining her triplets with water polo. But why get technical?

''Swam with her.'' Zack swallowed hard. ''Got…wet.''

''Usually do, swimming.''

Mindful of his blood pressure, Zack decided to ease back from that particular image. He'd save it for later. ''And you talked to her. Had conversations?''

"All the time. She's got a sharp brain. That sort of adds to the appeal, I think. After all, *I'm* not an animal."

"I'm just asking." It was a harmless diversion, Zack thought, for a happily married man who adored and lusted after his own wife. "You really met her." He sighed, lifted a crate of soft drinks.

"I not only met her. I kissed her."

"Get out of town."

"No, you're right, I didn't kiss her."

Zack snorted. "No kidding."

"*She* kissed *me.*" Nick leaned on a dolly of crates, tapping his finger to his lips. "She planted one on me. Right here."

"You're standing there telling me Chantel O'Hurley kissed you—on the mouth."

"Hey, would I lie to you?"

Zack thought about it. "No," he decided. "You wouldn't." Before Nick had a clue of his intention, Zack grabbed him, jerked him forward and kissed him—as Chantel had—full on the mouth.

"Damn it, Zack!" Another flurry of oaths followed as Nick grimaced and rubbed his mouth with the back of his hand. "Are you crazy?"

"Hey, I figure it's as close as I'll ever get." Satisfied, Zack carried in the next case. "A man has his dreams, pal."

"Well, keep your dreams away from me." Nick gave his mouth another swipe for good measure. "Man, what if somebody saw you do that?"

"Just us here, bro. And I do appreciate you coming in to give me a hand so soon after you got back in town.''

''Don't mention it. And I mean don't mention it.''

''So, how did Freddie like her trip to the rich and famous?''

''She's used to it.'' Nick scratched his neck as a line of sweat began to dribble. ''It's her kind of background.''

''I guess you're right. It's hard to tell. She's just Freddie around here.''

They finished unloading the cases, and finished off by having tall glasses of the iced tea Rio had stored in the refrigerator. ''Hot for June,'' Zack commented. ''You're going to have to hook the air conditioner up in the apartment.''

''Before long.''

It seemed a good opening, Zack mused, for something that had been preying on his mind. ''I was thinking, with the way your career's moving, and everything…'' *Everything* was Freddie, but it didn't seem quite the time to bring that up. ''You might not want to stay on here.''

''Upstairs?''

''Yeah, that, and here. Working at the bar.''

Puzzled, Nick set down his glass. ''Are you firing me?''

''Hell, no. The truth is, I don't know what I'd do without you right now. But I was beginning to worry that you're feeling obligated. Bartending wasn't your dream for your future.''

''It wasn't yours, either,'' Nick said quietly.

''That's different,'' Zack began, then shook his

head when he caught Nick's look. "Okay, maybe it wasn't. I had my shot, made my choice. And the fact is, I love this place. It makes me happy now. I don't want either one of us to lose sight of the fact that you've got something else going."

"Still looking out for me?"

"Habit."

Nick's lips curved. "Well, let's put it this way. Sooner or later you're going to have to find yourself another bartender and part-time piano player. But for the present, working the night shift doesn't interfere with my composing. And if the play's a bomb, I need a backup."

"It won't be a bomb."

"You're right, it won't. But let's just let things float the way they are for a while." He glanced at the clock, swore. "Damn, I'm late. I told Freddie we'd start a half hour ago. See you later."

Alone, Zack wandered back into the bar. No, he thought, it wasn't the deck of a ship, and he wasn't at the helm. And Rachel wasn't a blond movie queen.

He grinned and gulped down the rest of his iced tea. And he was a very, very happy man.

For another change of scenery, Nick had decided it was time they gave Freddie's piano a try. Despite the distractions, the noise and the temptation to spend their time playing, instead of working, while visiting the O'Hurleys, they had managed to buckle down long enough to make some real progress.

Nick's tendency might have been to float on that

for a day or two, but Freddie couldn't wait to get
back to it.

So they settled in her apartment for the afternoon,
putting the finishing touches on act 1's closing chorus number.

"It pops," Nick decided. "It's a good thing we
didn't finish this when Frank was around. He'd already be working on the choreography."

"Well, I like it. But I think—"

"Nope, time to stop thinking." He snagged her,
pulling her into his arms as he rose.

"Put me down. We haven't even started on the
opening for act 2."

"Tomorrow."

"Today," she said, laughing as she tried to wig-
gle free. "Nick, it's the middle of the day."

"Even better."

"You're the one who always says we have work
to do."

"That was when I was trying to avoid doing just
what I'm going to do right now." He dropped her
onto the bed, from a height designed to make her
bounce.

"We haven't finished our quota for the day."
When he grinned at her and began to unbutton his
shirt, she pushed herself up. "That's not the quota
I meant."

"Going to make me seduce you, huh?"

"No." Instantly, she thought better of it. Tilting
her head, she gave him a long, considering look.
"Well, maybe...if you think you can."

He'd already unbuttoned his shirt. The idea of a

challenge put a new spin on the easy pleasure he'd anticipated. She slid her gaze away, then back to him when he sat on the side of the bed.

"Just looking at me isn't very seductive."

"I like looking at you, now and again."

Her brows lowered even as he smiled. "That's very smooth, Mr. Romance."

"You have to remember, you're not really my type—according to an unimpeachable source." He merely caught her around the waist and pinned her when she started to spring off the bed in a huff.

"I'm not interested," she said coolly. "Let me up."

"Oh, you're interested. This little pulse in your throat..." He lowered his lips to it, grazed over. "It's hammering."

"That's annoyance."

"No. When you're really annoyed, you get this line right here." With a fingertip, he traced between her brows, smiling when the line formed. "Yeah, like that." He kissed her forehead, as well, satisfied when it smoothed.

"I don't want you to—" Her words slipped down her throat when his mouth cruised teasingly over hers.

"What?"

"To...mmmm."

"That's what I thought."

How could any man resist that slow melt she did? That quiet purr in the back of her throat when a kiss drew out, long and lazy?

And it was that way he wanted to make love with

her now. Lazily, so that his system could absorb every small and subtle change in hers. A touch, and she shifted to him. A murmur, and she sighed out her pleasure.

It seemed there was nothing he could do, or ask, that she didn't respond to willingly.

He wanted to see her, all of her, while the sun streamed in the windows and the spurting sound of midday traffic rattled against the panes. His hands were patient and slow as he flicked open the buttons of her blouse, one by one.

Beneath, she wore clinging cotton, with a fuss of lace at the bodice. He traced a fingertip along the edge, dipped under it, while her breath caught and quickened.

It was always this way, she thought hazily. Effortless and lovely. Whether they came together frantic or teasing, quiet or with shock waves, it was always so simple.

So perfect.

She could feel her own arousal blossom inside her, like a rose, petal by petal. It was just that easy to open for him, to bring him to her so that their mouths met and their bodies fit.

The faint breeze from the open windows drifted over her, as lazily as his hands, so that her skin was warmed, then cooled, warmed, then cooled. Dreamlike, the sounds from the street below, the streak of sunlight, all faded into a background, a kind of stage set for the fantasy.

She arched to help him when he drew the cotton away, when he loosened her trousers. In concert, she slipped his open shirt from his shoulders, letting her hands glide along the wiry strength of his arms.

She wasn't sure when the pace began to quicken, or the heat to build. The underlying urgency seeped into her like a drug, then shot straight through her bloodstream.

Now she was clinging to him, moving frantically beneath him.

"I want you now, Nick." The explosive spurt of energy had her rolling over the bed, struggling, even as he struggled to possess.

The pleasure was suddenly dark, dangerous, careening from misty dreams into a rage of greed. The hunger stabbed, so sharp, so voracious, that both of them shuddered.

No one had ever given him this.

"Now," she said, gasping out the word as she mounted him, crying out in triumph as she enclosed him.

Stunned by the lightning change in her, staggered by the force of his own appetite, he gripped her hips hard and let her ride him.

It was later when he thought of it. Later when they lay together, exhausted as children after a romp. He'd never given her the slightest hint of romance. None of the pretty trappings—the candles and wine, the quiet corners and long walks.

She deserved better. Then again, he'd tried to convince her right from the start that she deserved better than what he had to offer. Since she hadn't listened, the least he could do was give her something back.

He wished he could give her everything.

Where had that thought come from? he wondered, and let out a quiet, careful breath. Emotion whirled through him, buffeting him like a storm, he thought. Warming him like light. Calling to him like music.

When had he gone from enjoying her to craving her? To loving her?

Back up, back up, he warned himself. It would be disastrous for both of them if he let whatever was bubbling inside him get out of control.

Better to move on the initial idea, he decided, and pretend he'd never thought any farther than giving her a special evening.

"You've got a lot of fancy duds in that closet."

It amused her that he would have taken notice of her wardrobe. "Even in West Virginia, we manage to shop, and wear something other than overalls occasionally."

"Don't get testy—I like West Virginia."

It was where she'd grown up, in a big house, with antique furniture and a live-in housekeeper. And he'd grown up over a bar, and on the streets, with a stepfather who liked his whiskey just a little too much. Best to remember that, LeBeck, before you get any crazy ideas.

"I was just thinking you could pick out something jazzy, and we'd go out."

"Go out?" Intrigued now, she sat up, blinking sleepily. "Where?"

"Wherever you like." He wished she wouldn't look at him as if he'd just conked her on the head with a bat. They'd gone out before. More or less.

"I've got some connections, I could get tickets for a show. Not mine," he added before she could speak. "I don't want my own tunes competing inside my head."

She shifted again, foolishly delighted by the idea of a date. "It's kind of late in the day to snag tickets for anything."

"Not if you know who to call." He trailed a finger lightly down her arm in a way that made her want to sigh. She wondered if he knew he touched her just like that now and again, without thinking about it. "We could have a late supper afterward. At that French place you like."

Not just a date, she thought, dazed. A power date. "That would be nice." She wasn't sure how to react, and before she could, he was up and tugging on his clothes. "Get spruced up, then. I'll go make some calls and meet you at my place. An hour."

He leaned over to give her a quick kiss, then was gone, leaving her staring after him.

Maybe he wasn't Sir Lancelot, she thought with a shake of her head. But, tarnished armor or not, he had his moments.

It took her every bit of an hour to pull herself together. She hoped Nick would consider the off-the-shoulder plum silk jazzy enough. She did wish they'd arranged to meet at her place, however, when she narrowly avoided getting her heel caught in the sidewalk.

She breezed past Rio with a wave, and a quick

pirouette when he whistled at her. A quick knock at the top of the stairs, and she walked in.

"This time you're late," she called out.

"Had to help Zack with a delivery."

"Oh." She nibbled on her lip. "I didn't even think about your shift."

"It's my night off." He strolled out of the bedroom, still tugging on his jacket. He gave her a long look and a nod of approval. "Very nice."

"You've got such a way with compliments, Nicholas."

"How about this?" He grabbed her, lifted her to her toes and kissed her until her head threatened to blow off her shoulders.

"Okay," she said when she could breathe again. "That's pretty good."

Abruptly nervous, he let her go again. "We've got enough time before curtain for a drink. Why don't I play your personal bartender?"

"Why don't you, then? A little white wine—bartender's choice."

"I think I've got something you'll approve of." He'd snagged the bottle of Cristal from Zack's stash.

"Well." Freddie's eyes widened. "This is certainly turning into a night to remember."

"That's the idea." He decided he liked surprising her. Doing something out of the ordinary for her. He popped the cork with an expert's flourish, and poured it into two flutes he'd commandeered from the bar. "To family ties," he said, and touched his glass to hers.

She smiled as she lifted her own glass. "What

kind of a mood are you in? I can't quite pin it down.''

That stirring was going on again, needs and longings tangling together in his stomach, just around his heart. ''I'm not so sure myself.''

And the fact that he wasn't didn't make him as nervous as it should have. Because he was happy. Incredibly, completely happy. And he only got happier every time he looked at her.

He was certain he could go on looking at her for a lifetime.

And when that unexpected curve rounded like a fastball in his stomach, his breath caught and wheezed out slowly.

''Are you all right?'' Solicitous, Freddie thumped him on the back.

''I'm fine.'' *Love. A lifetime.* ''I'm...fine.''

Now it was her turn for nerves, so she took a small step back. ''Why are you looking at me like that?''

''Like what?''

''Like you've never seen me before.''

''I don't know.'' But that was a lie. He hadn't seen her before, not through the eyes of a man flustered by love.

He had, he realized, done the most amazing thing. He'd fallen head over heels in love with his closest friend.

''Let's sit down.'' He needed to.

''All right.'' Cautious, she settled on the sofa. ''Nick, if you're not feeling well, we can take a rain check on the show.''

"No, I'm fine. Didn't I say I was fine?"

"You don't look fine. You're pale."

He supposed he was. He'd never been in love before. He'd danced around it, toyed with it, teased the edges of it. But now it looked as though he'd fallen headfirst into the pit.

With Fred.

He was just getting used to the fact that he could make love to her. But being in love was going to take a lot more thought. It was a pity he couldn't wrap his brain around anything that wasn't sheer emotion.

"Fred...things have moved pretty fast between us."

She lifted a brow. "Do you call a decade-plus fast?"

He waved that away. "You know what I mean. I was thinking that I might be hemming you in, between the work and everything else."

The shiver that ran up her spine was icy and full of fear. But her voice was calm enough. "Are you trying to let me down gently, Nick?"

"No." The very thought appalled him. Losing her now—it was unthinkable. "No," he repeated, and gripped her hand so tightly she jolted. "I want you, Fred. I'm just beginning to realize how much."

Her heart turned slowly over in her breast, and swelled. "You have me, Nick," she said quietly. "You always have."

"Things have changed." He wasn't sure how to phrase it, not in a way that would satisfy them both. But he had to let her know something of what he was feeling. "Not just because we've gone to bed together. Not just because what I have with you there is different, stronger than anything I've ever had before."

"Nick." Swamped with love, she lifted their joined hands to her cheek. "You've never said anything like that to me before. I never thought you would."

Neither had he. Now, all at once, he was afraid he wouldn't get the words, the right ones, out fast enough. "I don't want to push things, Fred, for either of us, but I think you should know—"

The thud of heavy footsteps on the stairs had Nick swearing and Freddie cursing fate. Neither of them moved when Rio opened the door, looking grim.

"Nick, you'd better come downstairs."

A hard fist of fear rammed into his throat. "Zack?"

"No, it's not Zack." Rio glanced apologetically at Fred. "But you'd better come."

"Stay here," Nick ordered Fred, but Rio countermanded him.

"No, she should come, too. She can help." As Nick passed him, Rio clamped a hand on his shoulder. "It's Marla."

Nick hesitated, looked back at Freddie. There was no way to keep her out of it. "How bad is she?"

Rio only shook his head and waited for Nick and Freddie to precede him.

The name meant nothing to Freddie. She thought it might be some old flame who'd stormed into the bar in a jealous or, worse, drunken rage.

But the tableau that greeted hcr in the kitchen wiped that image out of her head.

The woman was dark, thin, and had probably been pretty once, before trouble and fatigue dug lines into her face. But it was hard to tell much of anything, because of the bruises.

She sat absolutely still, a young, hollow-eyed boy gripping the back of her chair, a smaller girl sitting at her feet, with her thumb in her mouth. In the woman's lap, a baby of perhaps three months cried thinly.

Nick wanted to shout at her, to rage. He wanted to shake this woman, this girl he had once known and nearly loved, until she lost that empty, hopelessly beaten look. Instead, he went to her, gently lifted her chin. The first tear spilled over onto her cheek as she looked at him.

"I'm sorry, Nick. I'm so sorry. I didn't know where else to go."

"You never have to be sorry for coming here. Hey, Carlo." He tried a smile on the boy. Though he laid a hand very lightly on the boy's shoulders, Carlo still stiffened and drew inward.

Big hands, the child knew, were never to be trusted.

"And who's this big girl. Is this Jenny?" Nick picked the girl up, set her on his hip. With her thumb still in her mouth, she rested her head on his shoulder.

"Rio, why don't you grill up some burgers for the kids?"

"Already on."

"Jenny, want to sit on the counter and watch Rio cook?" When she nodded, Nick settled her there. It only took a look to have Carlo creeping over, and out of the way.

"I don't want to be any trouble to you, Nick," Marla began, rousing herself to rock the baby.

"Want some coffee?" Without waiting for her assent, he walked to the pot. "The baby's hungry, Marla."

"I know." With what seemed like a terrible effort, she shifted, reaching for the paper bag at her feet. "I can't nurse her. I'm dried up. But I got some formula."

"Why don't I fix it?" With a bolstering smile, Freddie held out her arms. "Is it all right if I hold her?"

"Sure. She's a good baby, really. It's just that..." She trailed off and began to weep without a sound.

"You're going to be all right now," Freddie murmured as she slipped the baby out of Marla's hold. "Everything's going to be all right now."

"I'm so tired," Marla managed. "It's just that I'm tired."

"Don't." The order was quick and harsh as Nick set the coffee in front of her. "He knocked you around again, didn't he?"

"Nick." Freddie sent a warning glance at the children.

"You think they don't know what's going on?" But he lowered his voice. "Welcome to reality." He sat beside Marla, took her hands and set them around the cup. "Are you going to call the cops this time?"

"I can't, Nick." His snort of disgust seemed to shrink her. "I don't know what he'd do if I did. He gets crazy, Nick. You know how crazy Reece gets when he's drinking."

"Yeah." Absently he rubbed a hand over his chest. He had the scars to remind him. "You told me you were going to leave him, Marla."

"I did. I swear I did. I wouldn't lie to you, Nick. I've been in that apartment you helped me get before the baby was born. I wouldn't take him back, not after the last time."

The last time, Nick recalled, Reece had knocked her down the stairs. She'd been six months pregnant.

"So how'd you get the split lip, the black eye?"

She looked wearily down at her coffee, lifted it mechanically to drink. Rio set a plate in front of her.

"I'm going to take the kids inside to eat."

"Thanks." She swiped at another tear. "You two be good, you hear? Don't make any trouble for Mr. Rio." She nearly smiled as Freddie sat down to feed the baby. "Her name's Dorothy—like in *The Wizard of Oz*. The kids picked it out."

"She's a lovely baby."

"Good as gold. Hardly ever cries, and sleeps right through the night."

Nick interrupted her, patience straining. "Marla."

In response, Marla took one shuddering breath. "He's been calling me, wanting to see the kids, he said."

"He doesn't give a damn about those kids."

"I know it." Marla's lip trembled, but she managed to firm it. "So do they. But he sounded so sad on the phone, and he came by once and bought them ice cream. So I hoped, maybe, this time…"

She trailed off, knowing that hope was more than foolish. It was deadly.

"I wasn't going to take him back, or anything. It just seemed as if I should let him see the kids now and again. As long as I was right there to make sure he didn't drink or get mean. But tonight, when he came around, I was in the bedroom with the baby, and Jenny let him in. It was too late, Nick. I could see right away he was drunk, and I told him to get out. But it was too late."

"Okay. Take it slow." He rose to wrap some ice for her swollen lip.

But she couldn't take it slow, not now that it was pouring out of her. Like poison she'd been forced to drink. "He just started smashing things and screaming. I got the kids into the bedroom, got them away so he wouldn't hurt them. That only made him madder. So he went after me. I don't know how I got away from him, but I got into the bedroom with the kids, locked the doors. We got out by the fire escape. And we ran."

"Nick," Freddie murmured. "Take the baby." She rose, passing him the dozing infant. "Let's clean you up," she said briskly, and ran water on a cloth. With gentle hands, she smoothed it over Marla's face.

As she tried to soothe the bruises, clean the cuts, she talked softly. About Marla's children, caring for a new baby. When she felt Marla begin to respond, she sat again, took the woman's hand.

"There are places you can go. Safe places, for you and your children."

"She needs to call the cops." However fierce his voice, Nick cradled the sleeping baby tenderly on his shoulder.

"I don't disagree with him." Freddie picked up the wrapped ice, offered it to Marla. "But I think I understand being afraid. They'd help you at a women's shelter. Help your children."

"Nick said I should go before, but I thought it was better to handle it on my own."

"Everybody needs help sometime."

Marla closed her eyes and tried to find some tattered rag of courage. "I can't let him hurt my kids, not anymore. I'll go if you say it's right to, Nick."

It was more than he'd expected. He knew he owed part of the win to Freddie's quiet support. "Fred, upstairs, in the drawer under the kitchen phone, there's a number. It says *Karen* over it. Call it, ask for her, and explain the situation."

"All right." As she walked away, she heard Marla begin weeping again.

She'd hardly completed the arrangements when Nick came in.

He took a moment to study her—the slim woman in the elegant dress. "I'm going to dump on you, Fred. I'm sorry our whole evening is shot, and it's not over yet."

"It's all right, but I don't know what you mean. Oh, Nick, that poor woman."

His eyes only darkened. "I want you to take her and the kids to the shelter. They're not too happy having a man come around there in the first place. Small wonder. I'd feel better knowing you were with her, saw her settled in."

"Of course, I'd be glad to. I'll come back as soon as—"

"No, go home." The order snapped out. "Just go home when you're done. I've got something to do."

"But, Nick..."

"I don't have time to argue with you." He strode out, slamming the door behind him.

He had something to do, all right. And Nick figured it would take very little legwork to locate his old gang captain. Reece still ran in the same circles they had when they were teenagers. He still haunted the same streets and the same dingy rooms where a few dollars would buy anyone of any age drugs, liquor or a woman.

He found Reece huddled over a whiskey in a dive less than fifteen blocks from Lower the Boom.

The atmosphere wasn't designed to draw a discerning clientele. The air was choked with smoke and grease, the floors littered with butts and peanut shells. And the drinks were as cheap as the single hooker at the end of the bar, staring glassily into her gin.

"Reece."

He'd put on weight over the years. Not the muscle of maturity, but the heaviness of the drunk. He turned slowly on the stool, the sneer already in his eyes before it twisted his mouth.

"Well, well, if it isn't the upstanding LeBeck. Bring my friend a gentleman's drink, Gus, and hit me again. Put 'em both on his tab." The thought struck Reece so funny, he nearly rolled off the stool.

"Save it," Nick told the bartender.

"Too good to have a drink with an old friend, LeBeck?"

"I don't drink with people who shoot me, Reece."

"Hey, I wasn't aiming at you." Reece tossed back his whiskey and slapped the empty glass on the bar as a signal for another. "And I served my time, remember? Five years, three months, ten days." He took out a crumpled pack of cigarettes and pulled one out with his teeth. "You're not still sore I hooked up with Marla, are you? She always had a thing for me, old buddy. Hell, I was doing her back when you thought she was your one and only."

"A smart man learns to forget about yesterday, Reece. But you were never too smart. But it's Marla we're going to deal with. Here and now."

"My old lady's my business. So are the brats."

"Was, maybe." The wolf was in Nick's eyes now, as he leaned closer to Reece. And the wolf had fangs. "You're not going near them again. Ever. If you do, I'll have to kill you." It was said quietly, with a casualness that made the bartender check for his Louisville Slugger, just under the cash register.

Reece only snorted. He remembered Nick from the old days. He'd never had the guts to follow through on a threat with any real meat. "The bitch come running to you again?"

"I guess you figure she got off easy—a split lip, a few bruises. She didn't have to go into the hospital this time."

"A man's got a right to show his wife who's in charge." Brooding over it, Reece swirled his liquor. "She's always asking for it. She knew I didn't want that last brat. Hell, the first one ain't even mine, but I took her on, didn't I? Her and that damn little bastard. So don't you come around telling me I can't teach my own woman what's what."

"I'm not going to tell you. I'm going to show you." Nick rose. "Stand up, Reece."

Reece's reddened eyes began to gleam at the possibility of spilling blood. "Going to take me on, bro?"

"Stand up," Nick repeated. Seeing the bartender make a move out of the corner of his eye, Nick reached for his wallet. He pulled out bills, tossed them on the bar. "That should cover the damages."

The bartender scooped up the money, counted it and nodded. "I got no problem with that."

"You've been needing the high-and-mighty beat out of you, LeBeck." Reece slid off his stool, crouched. "I'm just the one to do it."

It wasn't pretty. At first blood, the hooker deserted her gin and crept out the door. The few others who inhabited the bar stood back and prepared to enjoy.

Drunk he might be, but the whiskey only made Reece more vicious. His meaty fist caught Nick at the temple, shooting jagged lights behind his eyes, and then another fist plowed into his gut. Nick doubled over, but as he came up again, his fist drove hard into Reece's jaw.

He followed through methodically, cold-bloodedly, concentrating on the face. Blood spurted out of Reece's nose as he tumbled back against a table. Wood splintered under his weight.

With a roar of outrage, Reece charged Nick like a bull, head lowered, fists pumping. Nick evaded the first rush, landed a fresh blow. But in the narrow confines of the bar, there was little room to maneuver. Outweighed, he went down hard under Reece's lunge.

He felt Reece's hands around his neck, choking off air. Ears buzzing, he pried at them, sucking in air and gathering strength to drive a short-armed punch. Reece's teeth tore his knuckles, but he continued to hammer, almost blindly now, until the stranglehold loosened.

There was an animal in him. It eyed Reece ferally, wrestled the bigger man over the floor. There was the sound of smashed glass, the sting of it pricking and biting at skin. Hate made him strong and wild and merciless.

He could smell the blood, and taste it. Even as Reece's eyes rolled back and his body sagged, Nick continued to pound.

"Enough." It took the bartenders and two others to drag Nick up. "I don't want nobody beat to death in my place. You done what you come to do, now get out."

Nick staggered once, wiped the blood off his mouth with the back of his hand. "You tell him when he comes to, if he raises his hand to a woman again, I'll finish the job."

Chapter Eleven

Freddie considered going home after delivering Marla and her family to the abuse shelter. God knew she was drained, as emotionally and physically exhausted as she'd ever been in her life. She'd gone no farther than the entryway of the shelter herself, but she'd been relieved that it didn't seem like an institution.

Nick had done his research well.

There'd been children's drawings tacked up on the wall, and a small sitting room off to the side, where the furnishings were spare, but comforting.

The woman who greeted them had seemed weary, yet her voice had been soothing. Freddie's last glimpse of Marla had been watching her being led up the stairs, with the woman murmuring to her.

So she didn't go home, despite Nick's insistence, but went back to wait for him.

"Figured you'd be back," Rio said when she stepped into the kitchen. "You got Marla and the kids away okay?"

"Yes." She sat, let her shoulders sag against the chair. "It seemed like a good place. A safe one. I don't think she even realized where she was. She just followed along, like the children."

"You've done all you can do." Rio set a plate in front of her. "You eat something now. No arguments."

"I won't give you any." Freddie picked up her fork and dipped into the chicken and rice. "Who is she, Rio?"

"A girl Nick used to know. He didn't see much of her for a while, after he got settled down here with Zack and Rachel. When she got pregnant with the boy, Carlo, her family booted her out."

"Heartless," Freddie murmured. "How can people be so heartless? What about the father?"

"Wasn't interested, I guess." Rio shrugged, caught himself and turned to her. "The boy isn't Nick's."

"You don't have to tell me that, Rio. He'd never have left them to fend for themselves." Setting her fork aside, she rubbed her hands over her face. "This man, the one who did this to her. He isn't Carlo's father?"

"Nope. She didn't get tangled up with him until about four years ago. He was doing time when the boy was born."

"A real prince."

"Oh, Reece is a royal bastard, all right." Rather than the coffee she'd expected, Rio set a cup of herbal tea in front of her. "I guess the name isn't ringing any bells with you."

"No." She frowned, sniffed the tea. Chamomile. It almost made her smile. "Should it?"

"He nearly killed Nick." Rio's dark eyes went grim. "A little over ten years ago, he broke in here with a couple of his Cobra slime buddies, juiced up and armed to the teeth. Figured on robbing the place. He was going to shoot Zack."

The blood drained out of her face. "I remember. Oh, God, I remember. Nick pushed Zack away."

"And took the bullet," Rio finished. "I thought we were going to lose him. But he's tough. Nick's always been tough."

Very slowly, as if her bones might shatter from the movement, she rose. "Where is he, Rio? Where's Nick?"

He could have lied to her. But he chose to tell her straight. "I gotta figure he went looking for Reece. And I gotta figure he found him."

She had to fight to get the air out of her lungs, to pull it back again. "We have to tell Zack. We have to—"

"Zack's out looking right now. So's Alex." He set a huge and gentle hand on her shoulder. "There's nothing to do but wait, honey."

So she waited, eventually going upstairs to pace Nick's apartment. Every sound on the street, from the bar below, had her holding her breath. Every wail of a siren had her trembling.

He's tough. Nick's always been tough.

She didn't give a damn how tough he was. She wanted him home, whole and safe.

Tormented by the images rolling through her brain, she kept her hands busy. She began to tidy the room, then to dust, then to scrub.

When she heard footsteps on the stairs, she was down on her knees washing the kitchen floor. She scrambled up, raced toward the door.

"Nick. Oh, God, Nick." All but shattered with relief, she threw her arms around him.

He let her cling for a moment, though the pressure had the aches in his body singing. When he found the energy, he peeled her away.

"I told you to go home, Fred."

"I don't care what you told me, I was— Oh, you're hurt."

Her eyes went huge as relief jerked into shock. His face was bloody, one eye nearly swollen shut. His clothes were torn and stained with more blood.

"You need to go to the hospital."

"I don't need a damn hospital." He lurched away from her, gave in to his weakened legs and sank into a chair. And prayed to any god that might be listening that he wouldn't be sick. "Don't start on me. I've already been through this with Zack. Go away, Fred."

Instead, she said nothing, walked into the bathroom and gathered up every first aid supply she could find. Armed with antiseptic, bandages and dampened cloths, she came back to find him sitting as she'd left him.

He took one look, would have scowled if his face hadn't felt as though it would crack open at the movement. "I don't want you nursing me."

"Just be quiet." Her hands were a great deal steadier than her voice when she dabbed at the blood. "I imagine I'm supposed to ask how the other guy looks. You had no business going after him."

"It is my business. She meant something to me once." He hissed, then settled, when she pressed the cool cloth to his swollen eye. "And even if I'd never seen her before, any man who knocks a woman around, tosses kids around, deserves a beating."

"I don't disagree with the sentiment," she murmured. "Only with your method. This is going to sting some."

More than some, he discovered, and swore ripely. "I wish to hell you'd go away."

"Well, I'm not." She tried to comfort herself with the thought that the cuts on his face weren't deep enough for stitches. Then she saw his hands. White-hot fury erupted inside her. "Your hands. Look what you've done to your hands. You idiot. Why can't you use your head instead of your glands?"

She could have wept with grief. His beautiful, talented artist's hands were torn and bleeding. Dark, ugly bruises had already formed, marring them, swelling them.

"They ran into his teeth a few times."

"Isn't that just like you? Isn't that just typical? Nicholas LeBeck's first rule of order. If you can't solve the problem, batter it down." She was wrapping cold cloths around his hands as she spoke. "You could have called Alex."

"Don't hassle me, Fred. You heard her. She isn't going to file charges."

"She's in the shelter, isn't she? She and the children?"

"And he just walks? Not this time." Experimentally Nick flexed his fingers. They were stiff and painful, but it was the torso Freddie had yet to see that was agonizing. "He tried to kill my brother once, and did less than six years for it. The system says he's rehabilitated, so he gets out and starts hammering on Marla. So, screw the system. My way works."

"He nearly killed you before." Her lips trembled as she rose. "He could have done it again."

"He didn't, did he? Now back off."

He dragged himself to his feet and limped into the kitchen. He managed to locate the aspirin quickly enough, but with his injured hands he found he couldn't pry off the lid.

Her own movements stiff from a different kind of pain, Freddie took the bottle from him. She opened it, set it on the counter for him, then poured him a glass of water.

"How far, Nick?" Her voice was controlled, too controlled. "How far do you want me to back off?"

He didn't turn, only stayed where he was, his hands braced on the counter, his body throbbing with a thousand hurts. "I can't talk about this now. If you want to do something for me, you'll go home. Leave me alone. I don't want you here."

"Fine. I should have remembered, the lone wolf prefers to slink off on his own to lick his wounds. I'll just leave you to it." As wounded as he now, she spun on her heel. She was halfway across the living room when Zack came in. Brushing an impatient hand over her damp cheek, she kept walking. "Be careful," she warned. "I think he's rabid."

"Freddie—" But she was moving fast, her heels already clattering on the stairs. Zack marched into the kitchen. "What did you do to make her cry?"

Nick only swore and dumped four aspirin on the counter. "Stay out of it." He winced as the water he swallowed burned his abused throat. "I'm not in the mood for company, Zack."

"You aren't getting company. Sit down, damn it, before you keel over."

That, at least, seemed like a reasonable idea. With careful movements, Nick lowered himself into a kitchen chair.

Standing back, Zack took a survey. Freddie had done some good, he supposed, but his brother still looked like the wrong end of a punching bag. "Did a number on you, didn't he?"

"He got in a few."

"Let's get what's left of that shirt off and take a look."

"I'm not much interested in seeing." But he couldn't drum up the energy to object as Zack began removing the torn material. Zack's slow, vicious oaths confirmed the worst. "That bad?"

"He got in more than a few. Damn it, Nick, did you have to go looking for trouble?"

"I didn't have to look far, did I?" He looked up then, met Zack's eyes coolly. "It was a long time coming. Now it's done."

Zack merely nodded, began to open cupboards. "Is that liniment still around here?"

"Someplace. Under the sink, maybe."

Once he located it, Zack came back to finish what Freddie had started. "You're going to feel worse tomorrow."

"Thanks, just what I needed to hear. Got a cigarette on you? I lost mine."

Zack took one out, lighted it, placed it between Nick's swollen fingers. "I hope he looks as bad as you."

"Oh, worse." The sour grin hurt. "A lot worse."

"That's something, then. I'm surprised you had the energy left to fight with Freddie."

"I wasn't fighting with her. I just wanted her out. She shouldn't have been around this. Any of it."

"Maybe not. But I'd say she can handle herself."

She was sure of it. It seemed clear after two days that Nick was determined to avoid her. Still licking his wounds, she imagined as she walked back from Nick's apartment yet again.

Still, she hadn't expected the locked door. Her only consolation was that Zack had assured her Nick was healing.

She was tired of worrying about him, she decided. And since work wasn't an option until his hands were better, she'd found other ways to fill her time.

She'd enjoyed taking toys over to the shelter more than anything else. Marla still seemed nervous and strained, but the children were already relaxing. The highlight of Freddie's day had been when the solemn-eyed Carlo smiled at her.

Time, she thought. They only needed time and care.

And what, she wondered, did Nick need? Apparently he didn't think it was Freddie Kimball. At least not at the moment. So she'd give him the distance he wanted right now. But sooner or later, she was going to get sick of standing back and waiting.

Love shouldn't be so complicated. She brooded, looking down at the sidewalk. It all had seemed so simple when she left home to come to New York. Everything she'd planned and hoped for had slowly come to be.

Now, because of some blip from his past, it was falling apart on her.

With a sigh, she opened the security door of her building. The sudden jab from behind had her stumbling. She would have fallen, if an arm hadn't come around her, jerking her back.

"Keep walking," the voice ordered. "And keep quiet. Feel that? It's a knife. You don't want me to use it."

Calm, she ordered herself. Don't panic. It was broad daylight. "There's money in my purse. You can have it."

"We'll talk about that. Open the elevator."

The idea of being closed in with him, with the knife, had her struggling. She bit back a cry when the blade pierced.

"Open the elevator or I'll cut you open right here."

Fighting to keep part of her mind cool, free from the panic that had her body shuddering, she obeyed. Once they were inside and moving, he shifted her, and she could see him.

The thin face, the glazed eyes. It was the man Nick had called Jack.

"You're a friend of Nick's." She managed to keep her voice level. "I was with him the night he gave you money. If you need more, I'll give it to you."

"You're going to give me more than money." Jack lifted the knife, running the flat of the blade over her cheek. "It's a matter of honor, baby."

"I don't understand." Her wild hope of rushing out ahead of him, screaming, when they reached her floor was smashed when he twisted her arm behind her back.

"Not a peep," he warned. "We're going to walk straight to your place, and I know which one it is. I've seen your light come on. Then you're going to unlock the door, and we'll go inside."

"Nick wouldn't want you to hurt me."

"Too bad about Nick. You pull anything out of that bag but your keys, baby, and you'll be bleeding."

She took out her keys, her movements deliberately sluggish. If she stalled long enough, someone would see. Someone would help.

"Move it." Jack yanked her arm higher, so that she whimpered when the last lock opened. He was sweating when he shoved her inside. "Now then, it's just you and me." He pushed her into a chair. "Nick shouldn't have gone after Reece. Once a Cobra, always a Cobra."

"Reece put you up to this." A new glimmer of hope tormented her. "Jack, you don't have to do this. Reece is just using you."

"Reece is my friend, my bro." His eyes began to glitter. "Lots of the others, they forgot what it was like in the old days. But not Reece. He keeps the faith."

Freddie might have felt pity—for surely the man *was* pitiful—if fear hadn't had its bony fingers clutched around her throat. "If you hurt me, you'll be the one to pay. Not Reece."

"Let me worry about that. Now take off your clothes."

Now the fear screamed in her eyes. Seeing it, Jack grinned. He was flying now. He'd used the money Reece had given him for a nice solid hit of coke.

"We might as well have a little fun first. Strip, baby. I've got a feeling Nick's picked himself another winner."

He would rape her, she thought, and as hideous as that was, she felt she could survive it. But she knew, in some cold corner of her brain, that he couldn't intend for her to survive. He would rape her, then he would kill her.

And he'd enjoy both.

"Please, don't hurt me." She let the terror ring in her voice. She would use it, to fight back.

"You do what I tell you, you're nice to me, nobody has to get hurt." He licked his lips. "Stand up and strip, or I'll have to start cutting you."

"Don't hurt me," she said again. She braced herself. She would need momentum, and a great deal of luck. If she didn't follow through, she wouldn't get a second chance. "I'll do anything you want. Anything."

"Bet. Now get up."

He gestured with the knife, grinned. She let her eyes slide toward the bedroom door, go wide. Jack was just stupid enough to follow her glance.

And she sprang.

The keys he hadn't bothered to take away from her were clamped between her tensed knuckles like daggers. Without a moment's hesitation or regret, she went straight for the eyes.

He screamed. She'd never heard a man scream like that, high and wild. With one hand clutching his eyes, he swung out blindly with the knife. With every ounce of her strength, Freddie struck him over the head with her prized art deco lamp.

The blade clattered to the floor as he crumpled. Breathing hard, she stared down at him for several seconds. As if in a dream, she walked to the phone.

"Uncle Alex? I need help."

She didn't faint. She'd been terrified she would, but she managed to follow Alex's instructions and leave the apartment. She was outside, swaying at the curb, when the first cop car pulled up.

Alex was thirty seconds behind it.

"You're all right? You're okay?" His arms came around her hard, and the veteran cop buried his face in her hair. "Did he hurt you, baby?"

"No. I don't think. I'm dizzy."

"Sit down, honey. Sit right here." He helped her to the building's stoop. "Head between the knees, that's a girl. Take it slow. Get upstairs," he ordered the uniform. "Get that lowlife out of my niece's apartment. Book him on assault with a deadly, attempted rape. I want the knife measured. If it's over the legal limit, slap him with that, too."

"He said Reece told him to," Freddie said dully.

"Don't worry, we'll take care of it. I'll take you to the hospital. I won't leave you alone there."

"I don't need the hospital." She lifted her head again. The wavering dizziness had passed, but she still felt oddly light-headed. "He cut me a little, I think." Testing, she brushed her fingers over her side, stared dumbly at the smear of red.

In a flash, she was cradled in Alex's arms. "The hospital," he said again.

"No, please. It's not deep. It stings some, but it's almost stopped bleeding. It just needs a bandage."

At the moment, he would have indulged her in anything. Still holding her, he looked up as two of his men carried out a limp and bleeding Jack.

He couldn't take her back upstairs, Alex thought. And he wanted her away from the perp and the crime scene. "Okay, honey. The bar's close by. I'll take you there, and we'll have a look. If I don't like what I see, your next stop's the ER."

"All right." She let her head rest on his shoulder, discovering that all she really wanted to do was sleep.

"This creep needs a doctor," one of the officers told Alex. "He needs one bad."

"Take him in, then, see that he gets fixed up. I want him in shape when I lock him in a cell."

All Freddie remembered from the short trip to Lower the Boom was Alex's soothing voice. It reminded her of being rocked when she was a child and had the chicken pox.

"I didn't let him hurt me, Uncle Alex."

"No, baby, you took care of yourself. Just let me take over now."

Rio let out a shout of alarm when Alex pushed the kitchen door open. "Sit her down, sit her down right here! Who hurt my baby? Who hurt my sweetheart? Nick!" He bellowed it out before either Alex or Freddie could answer. "Get your ass down here, now!" Moving like a bulldozer, he shoved open the door between the kitchen and bar. "Muldoon, I want the good brandy in here, pronto. You just sit easy, honey," he continued, in a voice that had lowered by several decibels and softened like silk.

"I'm all right, Rio. Really." Already soothed, she turned her face into the wide paw he'd laid on her cheek.

"Looks shallow." Alex sighed with relief. He'd expected the worst when he tugged Freddie's blouse out of her waistband to examine the cut. "We'll patch it up for you."

"What the hell's all the commotion?" Obviously annoyed by the shouted orders, Zack came in, holding a bottle of brandy. One look at Freddie had him darting over and crouching in a position that mirrored Alex's.

"Give her room to breathe." Though shaken, Rio snatched the bottle and poured a hefty two fingers into a tumbler. "Drink it down, Freddie."

She would have obeyed, if Nick hadn't come stalking down the stairs. His injured eye was more open than closed now, but a rainbow of bruises and scrapes had bloomed on his face.

When he saw her, the blood drained out of it.

"What happened? Were you in an accident? Fred, are you hurt?"

He snagged her free hand, nearly crushing the bones.

"Give her a minute," Alex ordered. "Drink the brandy, Freddie. Take your time."

"I'm okay." But the jolt of brandy as it hit her system cleared the fog and brought on the trembling.

"Is that blood?" Nick stared, horrified, at the stain on her blouse. "For God's sake, she's bleeding!"

"We're taking care of it." Alex took the antiseptic Rio passed him and dabbed it on gently. "I want you to come home with me, Freddie. When you're feeling better, I'll take your statement."

"I can do it now. I'd rather do it now."

"What do you mean, statement? Were you

mugged?'' Nick demanded. ''Damn it, Fred, how many times have I told you to be careful?''

''She wasn't mugged,'' Alex snapped out. ''Your old pal, Jack, wasn't interested in her money.''

As soon as he said it, Alex cursed himself. Pale as death, Nick dropped Freddie's hand and stepped back.

''Jack.'' As fury filled the hole shock had dug, his eyes turned to hard green slits. ''Where is he?''

''In custody. What's left of him.'' Alex stroked a hand over Freddie's hair before taking out a pad and switching into cop mode. ''Tell me from the beginning, everything you remember.''

''I was going home,'' she began.

Nick listened, the bitterness burning his throat, the impotence dragging at him.

Because of him, he thought. All of it. Every instant of terror she'd been through was because of him. His need to settle debts, to handle a problem his own way, could have cost Freddie her life.

''Then I called you,'' Freddie finished. ''I could see he was bleeding. His eyes...'' She had to swallow.

''Let me worry about him,'' Alex told her. ''I want you to put it all out of your mind for now. I'll go back to your place and get some things for you. You can stay with us as long as you like.''

''I appreciate that, really I do, but I need to go home.'' She took his hand before he could protest. ''I can't be afraid to stay in my own home, Uncle Alex. He'd have gotten to me then, don't you see? I'm not going to let that happen.''

"Hardhead." He kissed her gently. "If you change your mind, it only takes a call." He rose then, skimmed his gaze over the three men standing by. "You look after her. I've got to get to the station and take care of this." In a mute apology, he laid a hand on Nick's shoulder. "Make her rest. She'll listen to you."

When he left, Freddie felt three pairs of eyes on her. "I'm not going to fall apart," she said.

Nick said nothing, simply stepped to her, scooped her off the chair.

"I don't need to be carried."

"Shut up. Just shut up. I'm taking her upstairs. She's going to lie down."

"I can lie down at home."

Ignoring her, he started up the steps.

"You don't want me here." As if to complete the day, tears began to burn her eyes. "Do you think I can't tell you don't want me here?"

"Here's where you're staying." He carried her inside and straight to the bedroom. "You're going to rest until you get some color back in your face."

"I don't want to be with you."

A quick stab in the heart made him wince. But he couldn't blame her. "I'm going to leave you alone, don't worry." His voice was quiet, distant. "Don't fight me on this, Fred. Please."

He drew the rumpled spread over her, neglecting to take off her shoes. "I'm going downstairs." He stepped back, dipped his hands into his pockets. "Do you want anything? Want me to call Rachel, or one of the others?"

"No." She closed her eyes. Now that she was horizontal, she wasn't sure she could get up again. "I don't want anything."

"Try to sleep for a while." He moved over to tug down the shades on the window and plunged the room into soft gloom. "If you need anything, just call down to the bar."

She kept her eyes closed, wishing him to leave, willing it. Even when she heard the soft click of the door closing, she didn't open them again.

He hadn't offered the loving compassion Alex had, or the quick, forceful concern of Rio or Zack. Oh, he'd been angry, she thought, furious over what had nearly happened to her. She knew he cared. They'd been part of each other's lives for too long for him not to.

But he hadn't held her. Not the way she so desperately needed him to.

She wondered if he ever would.

Chapter Twelve

She hadn't thought she would sleep. It was a surprise to wake, groggy, in the half-light. Freddie wasn't certain if it was a good sign or a bad one that she remembered immediately, and clearly, what had happened and why she was alone in Nick's bed in the middle of the day.

Wincing a little as the bandage on her side pulled, she tossed the spread aside. She was unbearably thirsty, and the brandy she was only vaguely aware of having drunk had left her a head full of cotton.

At the kitchen sink, she filled a glass of water to the rim and drank it down. It was odd, and annoying, she thought, that she still felt so shaky. Then it occurred to her that she hadn't eaten since breakfast, and that hadn't been much of a meal.

Without much hope, she opened Nick's refrigerator. She had her choice of a chocolate bar and an apple. Feeling greedy, she took them both. She was just pouring another glass of water when Nick walked in, carrying a tray.

His heart lurched when he saw her standing there, so small, so delicate. And when he thought of what might have happened to her. In defense, he kept his voice neutral. "So, you're up."

"It appears so," she said in the same distant tone.

"Rio thought you might want to eat something." He set the tray on the table. "Your color's back."

"I'm fine."

"Like hell."

"I said I'm fine. You're the one who looks like he's been run over by a truck."

"I went looking for my fight," he said evenly. "You didn't. And we both know where the blame lands in this one."

"With Reece."

In an attempt to keep himself calm, he took out a cigarette. "Reece wouldn't have given two damns about you if it hadn't been for me. And if you hadn't been with me in the first place, Jack wouldn't have known where to find you."

She took a moment to steady herself. "So, I see, this is all about you. In your twisted logic, I was threatened with a knife and rape because I happened to have walked down the street with you one night."

The knife. Rape. It froze his blood. "There's nothing twisted about the logic. Reece wanted to pay me back, and he found a way. I can't do much about it, since Alex—"

"Do?" she repeated, interrupting him. "What would you do, Nick? Go beat Reece up again, pound on Jack? Is that supposed to make it come out right?"

"No. I can't make it come out right." And that was the worst of it. There was nothing he could do to change what had happened. Only what might happen next. He crushed out the cigarette he found he didn't want. "You and I have to settle things, though. I think you should work at home, when you feel up to it again. I can send the music over to you."

"What exactly does that mean?"

"Just what I said. I figure we've reached a point in the score where it's just as constructive, maybe more so, to work separately." His eyes shot to hers, hardened. "And I don't want you around here."

"I see." She needed her pride now, every ounce of it. "I take that to mean on both professional and personal levels."

"That's the idea. I'm sorry."

"Are you? Isn't that nice. 'Sorry, Fred, time's up.'" She whirled on him. "I've loved you all my life."

"I love you, too, and this is the best for both of us."

"I love you, too," she repeated, snagging him by the shirtfront. "How dare you come back with some watered-down pat-on-the-head response when I tell you that!"

Very slowly, very firmly, he pried her fingers from his shirt. "I made a mistake." He'd convinced himself of it. "And now I'm trying to fix it. I understand that you might get emotions confused with sex."

She shocked them both by slapping him, and putting her weight behind it. For a motionless moment, there was only the sound of her unsteady breathing. Then she exploded. "Do you think it was just sex? That what happened between us was just heat and flash? Damn you, it wasn't. You know it wasn't. Maybe it was the only way I could get to you, the only way I could think of. But it mattered, it all mattered. I worked every step of the way to make you see it, see me. I planned it out, step by step, until—"

"Planned?" He cut her off with one searing look. "You planned it? You came to New York, convinced me to work with you, had me take you to bed? And it was all part of some grand scheme?"

She opened her mouth, closed it again. It sounded so cold, so calculated, that way. It hadn't been, hadn't been meant to be. Not when you added love.

"I thought it through," she began.

"Oh, I bet you did." The slip had given him the outlet he needed for his rage and distance. "I bet you figured it all out in that sharp little head of yours. You wanted something, and did whatever it took to get it."

"Yes." She sat down now, weakened by shame. "I wanted you to love me."

"And what's the rest of the plan, Fred? Tricking me into marriage, family, white picket fences?"

"No. I wouldn't trick you."

"You wouldn't think of it that way, but that was the goal, wasn't it?"

"Close enough," she murmured.

"I can see it," he snarled out as he stormed around the kitchen. "Freddie's list of goals. Move to New York. Work with Nick. Sleep with Nick. Marry Nick. Raise a family. The perfect family," he added, in a tone that made her wince. "It would have to be perfect, right? You always want everything neat and tidy. Sorry to disappoint you. Not interested."

"That's clear enough." She started to rise, but he pressed a hand to her shoulder and held her down.

"You think it's that easy? I want you to take a look, a good long one, at what you were fishing for. I'm two steps away from the guy who held a knife on you. I know it. The family knows it—the family you're basing all these half-baked fantasies on. Isn't that the way you saw it, Fred? Like the Stanislaskis?"

"Why wouldn't I?" she tossed back, humiliated that she was close to tears. "Why wouldn't you?"

"Because I've been around, and you haven't. How many people do you think there are out there like them? You're using top-grade for your yardstick."

"There's nothing wrong with that. It works. It can work."

"For them. A few others. Is that what started cooking in your head when we were with the O'Hurleys? Another big, happy family?"

She lifted her chin. "It should prove my point. It can work."

"For them." He slapped his palms on the table, forcing her to stare into his face. "Take another look here. What's happened in the last few days is my world, Fred. Battered women, frightened kids, drunks who brawl in bars. Men who think rape is an entertaining pastime. And you want to start a family on that? You need to be committed."

"You're not responsible for what happened to Marla. Or to me."

"No?" His lip curled. "Look at the thread. I'm the thread. Maybe I've been pulled out of that whole world," he said. "But it only happened because of the family. What do you think they'd say if they knew I've been sleeping with you?"

"Don't be ridiculous. They love you."

"Yeah, they do. And I owe them, plenty. Do you think I'm going to pay them back by shacking up with you over a bar? Do you think I'm crazy enough to think about marriage and kids. Kids, for God's sake, where I come from? I don't even know who my father was. But I know who I am, and I'm not passing it on. I care about you, sure I do—enough to get you the hell out."

"You care," she said slowly, "so you're breaking it off."

"That's exactly right. I was out of my mind to let it get this far, and I nearly—" Now he broke off, remembering how close he'd come, only a few days before, to declaring himself. "What matters is, you worked on me, and I let things get temporarily out of hand. It ends here. For the sake of the family, we'll try to forget any of it happened.''

''Forget?''

''All of it. I'm not going to risk hurting you any more, and I sure as hell don't want to hurt the rest of the family. They're all I've got—the only people who ever wanted me or cared about me.''

''Poor, poor Nick,'' she said, with ice. ''Poor lost, unwanted Nick. You really think you're the only one who's faced that kind of rejection, or wondered just what lack might have been passed onto him. Well, it's time you learned to live with it. I have.''

''You don't know anything about it.''

''My mother never wanted me.''

''That's bull. Natasha's—''

''Not Mama,'' she said coldly. ''My biological mother.''

That stopped him. It was so easy to forget Spence had been married before. ''She died when you were a kid, a baby. You don't know how she felt.''

''I know exactly.'' There was no bitterness in her voice. That was what tugged at him. There was no emotion at all. ''Dad would have kept it from me. I doubt he has a clue I ever overheard him talking to his sister. Or with Mama. I was nothing more than a mistake she'd made, then decided to forget. She left me when I was an infant, without a second thought. And her blood's in me. That coldness, that callousness. But I've learned to live with it, and to overcome it.''

He couldn't imagine her harboring that kind of pain, that kind of doubt. ''I'm sorry. I didn't know.

No one's ever talked about her." He wished he could have held her then, offered comfort, until her body lost that uncharacteristic rigidity. He didn't dare offer her anything. "But that doesn't change what's here."

"No, it doesn't. You won't let anything change." Freddie was crying now, but the tears were hot, more of anger than of grief. "You knew I was in love with you. And you knew, in the end, I would have made any compromise, any adjustment, to make you happy. But you don't make compromises, Nick LeBeck."

"You're too upset to handle this now. I'm going to get you a cab."

"You're not going to get me a cab." She shoved at him. "You're not going to send me anywhere. I'll go when I'm ready to go, and I can take care of myself. I proved that today, didn't I? I don't need you."

She let the words hang, closed her eyes on them a moment. When she opened them again, they were fierce. "I don't need you. What a concept in my life. I can live without you, Nicholas, so you needn't worry that I'll come around mooning over you. I thought you could love me."

Her breath came out steady, strengthening her. "My mistake. You aren't capable of loving that way. I wanted so pitifully little from you. So pitifully little, I'm ashamed."

He couldn't stop himself from reaching out. "Fred."

"No, damn you, I'll finish this. Not once did you

ever tell me you loved me. Not the way a man tells a woman. And not once did you try to show me, except in bed. And that's not enough. Not one soft word. Not one. You couldn't even drum up the effort to pretend and tell me, even once, that you thought I was beautiful. No flowers, no music unless we made it for someone else. No candlelight dinners, except when I arranged them myself. I did all the courting, and that makes me pathetic. I was willing to settle for crumbs from you, and that's exactly what I got.''

''It wasn't like that.'' It appalled him that she should think so. ''Of course I think you're beautiful.''

''Now who's pathetic?'' she snapped back.

''If I didn't think about romance, it was because things got confused so fast.'' That was a lie, and he knew it. Yet he wondered why he was defending himself, why he felt such panic at the steely, disinterested look she sent him, when he'd been so hellbent on pushing her away. ''I can't give you what you need.''

''That's very clear. I'm better off without you. That's very clear, too. So, we'll do just as you suggested. We'll forget it.''

He put a hand on her arm as she started to walk out. ''Fred, wait a minute.''

''Don't touch me,'' she said, in such a low, furious voice that his fingers dropped. ''We'll finish our commitment to the musical. And we'll make polite conversation around the family. Other than that, I don't want to see you.''

"You live three damn blocks away," he called after her.

"That can be changed."

"Running home after all?"

She shot one frigid look over her shoulder. "Not on your life."

He thought about getting drunk. It was an easy escape, and would hurt no one but him. But he just couldn't work up any enthusiasm for it.

He got through the night, though he didn't sleep. The music he tried to write in the dawn hours was flat and empty.

He'd done what he needed to do, he told himself. So why was he so miserable?

She'd had no right to attack him. Not after she told him that everything that had happened since she'd come to New York was part of some plot. He was the victim here, and still he'd done his best to protect her in the end.

Imagine him, married, trying to raise kids. He snorted, then dropped into a chair, because the whole picture was suddenly so appealing.

Insane maybe, he mused, but appealing. A family of his own, a woman who loved him. Surely that was insane.

Insane or not, it was hopeless now. The woman who had walked out the day before didn't love him. All she felt for him was disdain.

Saw to that, didn't you, LeBeck? You idiot.

He'd had a shot. It was all so clear, now that it was over. He'd had a chance to love and be loved, to make a life with the only woman who had ever really meant anything to him.

How could he have been so stupid, so blind? It had always been her. If he had good news, she was the first one he wanted to share it with. If he was down, he knew it would only take her voice over the phone to bring him up again.

Friends. He supposed that was what had thrown him all along. They'd been friends. And when he felt more than friendship for her, he'd tried to block it, ignore it, deny it. He'd used every excuse available to hide the real one.

He hadn't believed he deserved her.

Even when their relationship changed, he'd held part of himself back. She'd been right. He'd never given her soft words. He'd never shared the reins of courtship.

Now he'd lost her.

He let his head fall back, closed his eyes. She was better off without him. He was sure of that. Had been sure.

The knock on the door had him springing up. She'd come back, was all he could think.

All the pleasure died from his face when he saw Rachel.

"Well, that's quite a greeting."

"Sorry." Dutifully he pecked her cheek. "I was… Nothing. What you are doing here?"

"Paying you a visit. I don't have to be in court for another couple of hours." She walked over to a chair, sat, gestured to another. "Sit down, Nick. I want to talk to you."

It was her lawyer's voice that put him on guard. "What's the problem?"

"You are, I believe. Sit." When he did, she laid a hand on his. "I love you."

"Yeah, I know. So?"

"I just wanted to get that out of the way, so I can tell you what an absolute jerk you are." The hand that had rested so gently over his balled into a fist and rapped his shoulder. "What a stupid, idiotic, inconsiderate, blind male boob you are."

"What's the deal?" he said between clenched teeth, as she'd squarely hit a spot that was still raw from Reece. He supposed he deserved the pain.

"I stayed with Freddie last night. She didn't want me to, but we ganged up on her."

"Oh." He let out a careful breath. "So how is she?"

"As far as the attack on her, she's holding up. As far as your attack, she's pretty hurt."

"Hold on. I didn't attack her."

"Objection overruled. I pried most of what happened out of her. It's bad enough that you've broken her heart, Nick, but to mess up your own life while you were at it takes real skill."

His defense mechanism clicked in before he could stop it. "Look, we slept together a few times. I realized it was a mistake and put the brakes on."

"Don't insult me, Nick," she said coolly. "Or Freddie. Or yourself."

He let his eyes close with an oath. The hell with it, he thought. The hell with defending himself, with pride, with anything else that blocked the way. "I love her, Rachel. I didn't realize how much, how bad it was, until she walked out the door.''

It was hard, but Rachel restrained herself from offering the comfort, the sympathy, that stirred inside her. ''Have you bothered to tell her you love her?''

''Not the way she needed. It's one of the things I neglected.''

''So I gathered.''

''I wasn't prepared for it.'' He pushed himself up to prowl the room. ''She had it all worked out in her head. One of her step-by-steps.''

''And you found that insulting,'' Rachel put in. ''Which proves you're a fool. Some more intelligent men might have found being found attractive and desirable by an attractive, desirable woman a compliment.''

''It threw me, okay? It all threw me. Everything I was feeling for her hit me like a wall. I didn't know it could be like this.''

''So to fix it, you tossed her out.''

''She walked.''

''Do you want her to keep on walking? She will. And if you dare tell me that you're not good enough, that you haven't got what it takes to make her happy, I'll really hit you next time. There's only part of the boy I got stuck with all those years ago left in you, Nick. And it's the best part.''

He wanted to believe it. He'd tried for more than a decade to make it true. ''I don't know if I can give her what she wants.''

''Then you won't,'' Rachel snapped back, without sympathy. "And she'll survive. She's cried herself dry, and she's purged most of the rage. The woman I left a little while ago was very controlled, and determined to forget you."

"I want her back." The thought wasn't as frightening as he'd assumed it would be. In fact, it felt incredibly right. "I want it all back."

"Then you'd better get to work, pal." She rose, took him by the shoulders and gave him a quick kiss on the cheek. "My money's on you, LeBeck."

Nick wasn't sure he'd take the bet himself. The odds were long, he decided as he carted his bags toward Freddie's building. It was going to take some pretty fancy footwork to squeeze an entire courtship into one crowded balcony scene.

Nick glanced up to the fifth floor of Freddie's apartment building, and headed for the fire escape.

"And where do you think you're going, Le-Beck?"

The beat cop Nick had known half his life strolled up, tapping his baton.

"How's it going, Officer Mooney?"

But the wily veteran eyed Nick's bags suspiciously. "My question was, where are *you* going?"

"I need a break here, Mooney."

"Do you now? Well, why don't you tell me about it?"

"See that window?" Nick pointed, waited until Mooney's eyes lifted and focused. "The woman I love lives up there."

"Captain Stanislaski's niece lives up there. And the girl's had a spot of trouble."

"I know. She's the one I'm in love with. She's a little annoyed with me at the moment."

"Do tell."

"I messed up, and I want to fix it. Look, she's not going to let me in the front."

"You think I'm going to let you climb up to the lady's window?"

Nick shifted his bags. "Mooney, how long have you known me?"

"Too long." But he smiled a little. "What have you got in mind?"

By the time Nick finished telling him, Mooney was grinning. "Tell you what I'm going to do, since I've watched you grow from a snot-nosed punk into an upstanding citizen. I'm going to stand right down here and let you give it your best shot. If the lady isn't receptive, you're coming right back down."

"Deal. Listen, it could take a little time. She's pretty stubborn."

"Aren't they all? I'll give you a leg up, boy."

With Mooney's help, Nick managed to yank down the ladder. After a climb that reminded him that his bruises were still very much around, he tapped on Freddie's window.

Moments later, she jerked it open.

Her eyes were a little swollen, and that cheered him. Even if the expression in them wasn't welcoming.

"Fred, I want to—"

She slammed the window down and flipped the lock.

"Strike one, Nick!" Mooney called up. A man came out of the bakery behind him and paused next to the cop.

"What's going on?"

"The boy up there's trying to charm the lady."

Nick prayed it was just temper. If she'd finally written him off, he'd lose everything that mattered. He only had to get her attention, he assured himself, and wiped a damp, nervous hand on his jeans. He pulled the flowers out first. They'd gotten a little crushed, but he didn't think she'd notice.

He rapped again, harder. "Open up, Fred. I brought you flowers. Look." More than a little desperate, he waved the bouquet when her face appeared on the other side of the glass. "Yellow roses, your favorite."

Her answer was to yank the drapes smartly shut.

"Strike two, Nick!"

"Shut up, Mooney," he muttered.

He was drawing a crowd now, but he ignored it as he pulled out his next weapon. After arranging the candles in their holders, he lighted them. He turned to the blank window and tried to pitch his voice loud enough so Fred would have to hear him, but not so loud that he'd get commentary from below.

"Hey, I've got candlelight out here, Fred.... Did I ever tell you how beautiful you look in candlelight? The way your eyes sparkle and your skin kind of glows? You look beautiful in any light, really, sunlight or moonlight. I should have told you that. I should have told you a lot of things.''

Nick shut his eyes a moment, took a breath. ''I was afraid I'd mess up and ruin your life, Fred, so I messed up anyway and nearly ruined both our lives.'' His hands were pressed against the window glass now, as if he could will her to open it. ''Let me fix it. I've got to fix it. Just let me tell you everything I should have told you. Like the way the smell of you haunts me. I breathe you for hours, even when you're not there, like you're inside me.''

''That's pretty good,'' Mooney noted to several people who'd stopped to watch. They all agreed with him.

''Open the window, Fred. I need to touch you.''

He wasn't even sure if she was listening. All he could see was the insulated barrier of draperies. He set up the portable keyboard, to the hoots and calls of encouragement of the crowd below.

''We wrote this song for each other, Fred, and I didn't even know it.''

He played the opening chord from ''It Was Ever You'' and, tossing pride away, sang.

He was into the second verse before she snapped the drapes aside and tossed up the window.

''Stop it,'' she demanded. ''You're making a fool out of yourself and embarrassing me. Now I want you to—''

''I love you.''

That stopped her. He saw tears swim into her eyes before she fought them back. ''I'm not putting myself through this again. Now go away.''

"I've always loved you, Freddie," he said quietly. "That's why there was never anyone else who meant anything, or could. I was wrong, stupid, to think I had to let you go. I need you to forgive me, Fred, to give me another chance, because there's nothing without you."

The first tear fell. "Oh, why are you doing this? I'd made up my mind."

"I should have done it a long time ago. Don't leave me, Fred. Give me a chance." Nick picked up the flowers again and offered them.

After a moment's hesitation, she took them. "It isn't just flowers, Nick. I was angry then. It's—"

"I was afraid to love you," he murmured. "Because it was so big, so huge, I thought it might swallow me whole. And I was afraid to show you."

Her gaze lifted from the flowers, held his. She'd once dreamed about seeing that look in his eyes. The tenderness, the strength, and the love. "I never wanted you to be anything but what you are, Nick."

"Come on out." His eyes never left hers when he held out his hand. "Welcome to my world."

She sniffled, then shook her head with a laugh. "All right, but we'll probably be arrested for arson."

"No problem. I've got a cop watching."

Even as she stepped out on the crowded platform, she looked down. Besides the uniform, there were several others in the audience. Someone waved at her.

"Nick, this is ridiculous. We can talk this through inside."

"I like it out here." She'd wanted romance. By God, he was going to give it to her. "And there's not much to talk about—just tell me you still love me."

"I do." Swamped with it, she lifted a hand to his cheek. "I do love you."

"Forgive me?"

"I wasn't going to. Ever. I was going to live without you, Nick."

"That's what I was afraid of." He laid a hand over the one resting on his cheek. "And now?"

"You haven't left me much choice." She brushed a tear away. "What were you thinking of, candles and music before noon?"

She'd already forgiven him, he realized, humbled. "I thought it was time I did the courting. Do you want me to go to the next step in my master plan?"

"I want to apologize about that."

"I hope you won't." He lifted her hand and kissed it, in a gesture that made her blink. "I intend to remind you, for the rest of your life, that you came gunning for me. I'm glad you did." He kissed her hand again. "I'm going to need a long time to show my gratitude." Watching her, he shifted and took a small box out of his pocket. "I'm hoping you'll give it to me. Marry me, Fred." He flipped the top on the box to reveal an elegantly simple, traditional diamond. "No one's ever loved you the way I do. No one ever will."

"Nick." She pressed her hand to her mouth. This wasn't a dream, she realized. Not a fantasy, not a stage in some careful plan. It was real and wrenching.

And perfect.

"Yes. Oh, yes." On a watery laugh, she threw herself into his arms.

"Looks like the boy hit a home run after all," Mooney observed. He gave himself the pleasure of watching the couple five stories up kiss as if they'd go on that way through eternity.

Then he tapped his stick. "Okay, let's move along. Give them some privacy."

Whistling, Mooney sauntered away. He glanced back once, smiled as he saw the pretty woman toss her bouquet high in the air.

Nick LeBeck, Mooney thought. The boy had come a long way.

Epilogue

BROADWAY RHYTHM

By Angela Browning

After last night's wildly successful opening of *First, Last and Always*, starring the luminous Maddy O'Hurley and the delicious Jason Craig, there's no doubt about these two stellar performers' niche on the Great White Way. The audience, including yours truly, adored them from the dynamic, colorful opening scene to the wryly romantic closing number. Miss O'Hurley in particular proved her range and scope in her captivating portrayal of Caroline from quirky ingenue to mature woman.

While these two stars and the inspired supporting cast lit up the stage, it was the music that drove the production. Take it from me—as of last night, Broadway has two new darlings. The team of Nicholas LeBeck and Frederica Kimball have created a score that soared and dipped, that raised the roof and touched the heart. Believe me, there were few dry eyes in the house last night when the two leads reprised the haunting "It Was Ever You." Notes and lyrics are certainly the heartbeat of any musical, and this heart pumped with fresh energy and spirit. Mr. LeBeck's debut score for *Last Stop* earned him rave reviews, and sang with potential. With *First, Last and Always* he's proven himself.

His partner is every bit his match. Miss Kimball's lyrics range from the gently poetic to the smugly cynical to the brashly funny, slipping so truly into LeBeck's notes that it's not possible to tell which came first. Like all great collaborations, this one appears seamless.

Perhaps this is due to the fact that the team of LeBeck and Kimball are not only musical partners, but newlyweds. Married only three months, the bride and groom had plenty of reason to smile after last

night's smash opening. I, for one, wish
them a long, happy and productive partnership.

"How many times are you going to read that?"

Freddie sighed. She sat cross-legged in the middle
of the rumpled bed, copies of all the early reviews
spread around her. And over Nick. Her hair had long
since fallen out of the sophisticated twist she'd worn
to the opening. The sleek black gown she'd spent
days shopping for was tossed carelessly on the
floor—where it had landed when Nick peeled it off
of her.

They'd come in giggling sometime past dawn,
high on celebratory champagne, success and healthy
lust.

"It was wonderful."

He grinned. "Thanks."

With a laugh, she swatted him with the newspaper
and watched her wedding ring glint in the sunlight
that streamed through the window. It still gave her
a wonderful jolt to see it on her finger. "Not that—
but that wasn't bad, either. The night," she said,
closing her eyes to bring it all back. "The crowds,
the people, the lights and music. The applause. God,
I loved the applause. Remember how people stood
up and cheered at the end of 'I'm Leaving You
First'?"

He folded his arms behind his head and continued
to grin. She looked so cute, so pretty, sitting there

in one of his T-shirts, her hair curling everywhere, her eyes glowing.

She looked so...his.

"Did they? I didn't notice."

"Sure. That's why you broke all the fingers in my hand squeezing it."

"I was just trying to keep you from leaping on stage and taking a bow."

"I felt like it," Freddie admitted. "I wanted to jump up and dance. They loved it, Nick. They loved what we made together."

"So did I. I loved sitting front-row center and hearing what we created over the bar on my old piano. And remembering what happened to us while we wrote the words and music."

She laid a hand over his, linked fingers. "It was the most exciting time of my life. And last night just made it all the more special. Everyone looked so wonderful. All the family. It was almost like our wedding day, with everyone dressed up and beaming. And you were almost as nervous."

"You were every bit as beautiful." Nick watched her color come up, her smile spread. She wasn't used to him remembering to tell her, he knew, or being able to say it so easily. "Mrs. LeBeck." He sat up to comb his fingers through her hair, to meet her mouth with his. "I love you."

"Nick." She pressed her cheek to his and held tight. "It's all so perfect. I knew it would be if I waited long enough. And somehow I know it's only going to get better. We're a team."

"And we're a hit. LeBeck and Kimball. Broadway's new darlings."

She chuckled, then nuzzled his neck. "You read it this time."

His hands had already slipped under the T-shirt. "Now?"

"After," she murmured, then with a laugh, rolled over the rave reviews with him.

* * * * *

If you enjoyed what you just read,
then we've got an offer you can't resist!

Take 2 bestselling love stories FREE!

Plus get a FREE surprise gift!

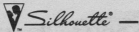

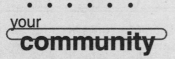
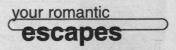